BEAUTY
and the
BEASTLY BILLIONAIRE

JUDY ANGELO

THE CASTILLOS
Book 1

BEAUTY AND THE BEASTLY BILLIONAIRE

*W*hat do you do when the man you end up working for is the worst bully you could ever imagine?

This is the dilemma facing **Ellie Goldwell**, one from which she would gladly walk away...except that she can't, not when her family is depending on her. She stands up for herself, though, letting her boss know that she is no pushover. After that, things look like they're under control...that is, until he demands that she accompany him to Argentina. It's here on his home turf where Ellie learns that, when it comes to matters of the heart, there's no such thing as...control.

Amadeo Castillo has never met a woman like Ellie Goldwell - feisty and defiant, a woman who will stand up to him, regardless of his position or power. He's used to being the one in the driver's seat - he even has the reputation of being a tyrant - but when Ellie enters the picture she becomes a challenge to his position, a threat to his reputation, and a hazard to his heart.

It's a brutal battle of will and wits, and all bets are off...

CHAPTER ONE

"Excuse me?"

"I said, come here." The man's voice was like granite, his dark eyes drilling into her, his stance rigid. And he'd said the words like she must not keep him waiting.

Ellie tilted her chin upward, determined not to show any hint of fear. She would stand up to this brute of a man even though he might be a good foot taller than she was. She would not be intimidated by anyone, regardless of who he was.

The man folded his arms across his chest and glared at her but he did not say another word. It was as if he thought that was enough to make her move.

She didn't budge.

"Do you want this job or not?" His tone was as harsh as the arctic. "Come over here so I can look at you." He jerked his head toward the huge bay window of the penthouse office suite. "In the natural light."

Ellie drew in her breath and then she tightened her lips. His question had done the trick. It was that word...job...that yanked her out of her mutiny and made her curl her fingers around her purse instead. The answer to his insolent question was yes, she wanted the job. She needed it. Desperately. And that was the only reason why she took one tentative step forward and then another...and another...until she was standing a mere three feet away from him.

The hardness in the man's glare gave way to a glint of triumph. "Closer." He said that one word and then he waited. He knew she would comply soon enough. It was so painfully obvious that he was the one in control.

Ellie cleared her throat. "How much closer do you want me to come? Can't you see me well enough from there?"

"No. I want you right here." He bit the words out then stabbed at a spot just a foot away from where he stood, his face darkening with impatience. At that moment he looked like, if she didn't move, he would make her.

So she moved. Ellie took that step that put her right by the window, exactly in front of him and there she stood, waiting for his next move. It was unnerving, being so close to this big, obviously powerful man. She felt out of her depth, like she should turn tail and run, but the agency had sent her. She was on the job. She couldn't back out now.

He caught her off guard, making her gasp when his hand suddenly shot out to cup her chin. She tried to step back, to escape his touch, but he didn't let her. All she could do was stand there, a prisoner to this man, the touch of his hand branding itself into her skin.

Seeming satisfied that he had her exactly where he wanted her, he turned her face toward the sunlight that streamed in through the window. His gray eyes intense and unreadable, he regarded her for mere seconds and then he let her go. "You'll do," he said and he was turning away before the words were even out of his mouth.

And his words, so casual and so dismissive, stung. You'll do? Ellie knew she'd been selected to attend this meeting at the head office of Aura Cosmetics because she was considered one of the best that Lord Modeling Agency could offer. And all he could say was, you'll do?

"Be back here tomorrow at ten. The photo shoot will be long and it will be demanding. Make sure you get enough rest tonight. I don't want you getting tired and messing up the shoot." The man was already back in his seat, not even sparing her a glance as he swiveled to face his computer screen.

For a moment Ellie didn't know what to do. That was it? She'd been in this man's office all of three minutes. He'd examined her and then dismissed her. And she still didn't even know his name.

"Excuse me," she said for the second time that morning but this time she was frowning. She was normally a placid soul but the man's rudeness was getting on her nerves. "Should I come here?" she asked. "To this office?"

He cut her a glance which clearly meant, are you still here? "Check in with the receptionist," he said, his voice brusque. "She will know where to send you."

"And whom should I ask for?" Two could play that game. Ellie could be just as cool, just as formal. She tilted her chin upward so she could look down her nose at him, literally. "We haven't been introduced."

That seemed to get his attention. The man's brows shot up and then they fell in a frown. "You don't know who I am?"

"No, I don't," she said in her best imitation of Queen Elizabeth II. Back at home in the Cayman Islands her friends at school always got a kick out of her play at royalty. It probably wouldn't have the same effect here but she would use it just the same.

The man pushed back in his chair and propped his elbows on the arms of his chair. "Who sent you up here?"

Glad she was finally commanding his full attention, Ellie lowered her chin and stared directly into his piercing eyes. "The agency told me I should meet with Jack Usher but as soon as we met he had his assistant deposit me here. Neither of them told me who you are."

"Hmm. Some creative director..." He'd grumbled under his breath but Ellie heard him. Obviously, he was not pleased. He looked up at her from where he sat by his desk and, as quickly as he'd moved earlier, he was up and striding to the window and back toward her. His movement, so lithe and determined, portrayed the latent power of a black panther, fearsome and fearless, ready to pounce on its prey.

He stuck his hand out, that same big, strong hand that had clasped her chin. "I am Amadeo Castillo," he said, "owner of Cosmeticos Aurora. I'm sorry my creative director was rude and did not tell you this."

His creative director was rude? Ellie almost laughed. And what about him? This man, Amadeo Castillo, hadn't been an example of gentility, either. He was still holding his hand out so there was nothing for Ellie to do but take it. The minute she did he wrapped his fingers around her hand, enveloping it in his grip, holding it like he owned that part of her person. Or owned her...

And, for some strange reason, her heart began to race. It was a simple act, taking her hand, but it was like, in doing so, he now had possession of more than just her hand. He had possession of her. And she didn't like it.

"And I am Ellie Goldwell," she said, struggling to keep her voice calm and just a little bit frosty. And she was not going to say she was pleased to meet him. He might be the owner of this billion-dollar company but she was not impressed, not if it made this man feel he was above being polite. She'd heard enough and now she was ready to go so she began to pull her hand from his grasp. At least, she tried. He did not let her go.

"Ellie Goldwell," he said and the way he said her name, each syllable rolling off his tongue, made her draw in a stealthy breath. If he'd been trying to sound like a modern-day Don Juan he was doing a heck of a job. "Lord Agency's top model. You will be the new face of Cosmeticos Aurora, Ellie Goldwell. I have spoken."

I have spoken? That called for a lifting of the eyebrows. She didn't even hide her surprised amusement.

"There is no need for that look, Miss Goldwell. This is a very important position. You will represent my company to the world. I have final say on who fills this significant role." It was after he'd made that declaration, his eyes filled with unmistakable pride, that he released her hand. "Now you must go. I told you to get your rest. Tomorrow you must be fresh and ready to work."

He was dismissing her again but Ellie did not acquiesce and turn toward the door like he obviously expected. She stayed right where she was and returned her hand to its previous position, clasping her purse in front of her like a shield. She tilted her head as she looked up at him. "I have a question," she said as he gazed down at her.

"A question." His brows lifted. "What question is that?"

"I was told to come to Aura Cosmetics of New York but you said your company is Cosmeticos Aurora. Twice. Are they one and the same?"

Amadeo Castillo smiled and for one brief moment he almost seemed human. It was a genuine smile, one that reached his eyes, those deep-gray eyes with thick, long lashes that would be the envy of any model. And his lips, so tight and firm just moments before, now curved in a way that made them seem so very kissable.

Ellie blinked. Where in the world was her mind taking her? She felt the heat of embarrassment begin to rise up her neck but she was rescued when the owner of the corporation began to speak.

"You have it right, Ellie Goldwell. They are one and the same." He nodded. "My company is based in Argentina and is called Cosmeticos Aurora. For my North American operation, though, it is called Aura Cosmetics. For the moment I am operating out of my New York office." And then, as quickly as his face had softened, it changed right back. "But now you must go," he said. "There is much I have to do today." And, just like that, he turned on his heel and headed toward his desk.

Taken aback by his abrupt departure, for a second Ellie did not move. Then, catching herself, she gave a quick shake of her head and turned toward the door. "Good day, Mr. Castillo." She threw the words, so cool and formal, over her shoulder as she went.

"The name is Amadeo," he said to her departing back. "That is what you must call me."

Ellie did not reply. As she opened the door and closed it firmly behind her she was frowning. What she must call him.

Must. As if she had no choice in the matter. She had a feeling that what he'd just said would set the tone for what was to come.

Amadeo Castillo was a man who expected his 'subjects' to jump at his command. The question was, could she swallow her pride and play that humiliating role? She already knew this man would be a trial and a half. She could only pray that, before the job was done, she didn't lose her cool and put him in his place.

She would have a task of it, biting her tongue. Heaven help her.

. . ❧ . .

"SPEAKING." AMADEO'S tone was brusque. He had no time for small talk, not when he was consumed by one of the grandest projects he'd decided to undertake since setting up offices in America two years earlier. His company was expanding at a rapid pace, a lot faster than he had expected, and it was taking his every waking moment to keep things on track.

"*Senor* Castillo, I am sorry to disturb you. This is Roberto Gonzalez from *Las Noticias Contemporaneas* in Buenos Aires. We have noted the remarkable success of your company, now considered one of the largest in Argentina. I will be in New York next Wednesday and wondered if I could meet with you for an interview."

Amadeo tightened his grip on the phone receiver. A reporter. Not what he needed just now. Publicity was good but he'd had enough of that lately, what with all the buzz around his move to rebrand Aura Cosmetics in America. He was deep in the middle of that major undertaking and the last thing he needed was distractions.

In a past life he would have rid himself of the journalist in a split second but now he paused. If the man could do his thing in thirty minutes or less he could spare him that much but not a minute more. If it would keep his brand top-of-mind in Argentina then it would be thirty minutes well spent. "Next Wednesday, eleven o'clock," he said into the phone. "You will have thirty minutes. Do not be late."

"Si, si. Of course, *Senor* Castillo. I will be there. I appreciate-"

"Speak with my secretary and book the appointment or you will lose that slot to someone else." Before the man could say another word Amadeo had hung up and was already dialing another number, this time from his cell phone, the conversation with the journalist already forgotten.

As soon as he heard the click that said Jack had picked up the call Amadeo began speaking. "It's three-thirty," he said, his voice cool. "It's been over four hours since you sent that model to my office. Why haven't you come up to see me?"

There was an audible gulp and then a swift intake of breath. "I'm sorry, Mr. Castillo...Amadeo...I got caught up in the preparations for tomorrow's photo shoot. And...I didn't know you expected me to meet with you."

For a moment Amadeo didn't say a word. He just let the man stew. When he finally spoke it was through gritted teeth. "You should know me by now. I expect follow-up on all projects, particularly this one. I must be debriefed on everything. I will be leaving in the next half hour. I will expect your full report before I go."

"But I'm in the middle of-"

"You have half an hour." Amadeo hung up the phone. He didn't give a damn what his creative director was in the middle of.

Within minutes, just like Amadeo expected, there was a tap at his door. "Enter." He sat back in his chair and waited for Jack to tentatively push it open and pop his head in to peer at him, just like he always did. Usher took a tentative step forward and then turned to close the door behind him. When he turned back to face Amadeo his face was flushed, like he'd hurried to get there. Looking like he wanted to be anywhere but there he slowly approached the chair and sank down onto the seat.

"So what do you think of her?"

"Uh, me? I think she's...right for the job?" Jack said the words like he was asking a question, his look uncertain.

"Do you think she is right for the job or don't you?"

"I'm...sorry. I sent her up to you because I think she's the right one for the job. Perfect." As he spoke his voice became stronger, more confident. "As soon as I saw Ellie Goldwell I knew she was the perfect face for Aura Cosmetics – vibrant and bold with just a hint of innocence to give her maximum appeal." He brought his closed-up fingers to his lips and kissed the tips. "Mmm. Magnificent. They will eat her up."

Amadeo's eyes narrowed. "But will she represent us well? You're the creative director. What do you think?"

"I wouldn't have sent her up to you if I didn't think she would. She's the one, Amadeo. Ellie Goldwell is the one." Jack's blue eyes shone and he leaned back in his chair, propped his elbows on the arm and tented his fingers in front of him. His enthusiasm overriding his nervousness, he now looked much more relaxed,.

Amadeo bit back a smile. His first name had slipped from Jack's lips so easily this time. If for no other reason, he knew that Ellie Goldwell had made a strong impression. She'd made Jack overcome his usual hesitation. He nodded. "I thought so. On this, we both agree. I was satisfied with her and that is why I told her to be here at ten o'clock for the photo shoot."

"Yes, she came down and told me you gave her the green light." Jack was grinning now. "You've made a good choice. You will not regret it."

"No, I will not," Amadeo said, full of confidence. "I am sure Miss Goldwell knows I expect professionalism. Perfection. If she does not deliver then she will be cut. Done." He slashed his hand across his neck to emphasize his point.

Suddenly, Jack didn't look quite so confident. He swallowed. "I'm sure she'll be superb."

"She'd better be." Amadeo narrowed his eyes. "I will expect nothing less."

CHAPTER TWO

It was almost seven by the time Ellie entered her apartment building that evening. When she'd left Aurora Cosmetics she'd gone to the pharmacy and then stopped at the supermarket and now, after lugging three bags of groceries all of seven blocks, she was dog-tired. What made it worse, the May evening had been excessively warm, making her perspire. When she got to the elevator she dropped the bags on the floor then slumped against the mirrored wall, glad she was the only one inside. The ride to the eleventh floor gave her just enough time to catch her breath and regain her strength and then the elevator door opened and she was off again, dragging the heavy bags down the hallway to apartment 1103.

She dropped the bags onto the floor again and, not bothering to dig in her purse for her keys, she rapped at the door. "Mom, I'm home." Within seconds she heard the patter of not one, but two pairs of feet running to the door. There was the clatter of the chain lock against the door and then it flew open to reveal two eager faces smiling up at her. She smiled back. "Hi, guys. Peter, can you take this bag? And you can grab my purse, Simone. Your big sis isn't as strong as she used to be."

Ellie chuckled as her eight-year-old sister rolled her eyes. The little girl shook her head as she reached out to pull Ellie's purse from her arm. "You always talk like you're so old," she grumbled. "You're only twenty-three. That's not old."

Ten-year-old Peter grabbed the grocery bag that was slipping from Ellie's numb fingers. As he turned with the bag of fruits and vegetables in hand he was grinning at Simone. "You'll be talking just like Ellie when you get that old. Girls get old real fast, you know."

"They do not." Simone glared at him. "Girls grow up just like boys do. We don't get old any faster than boys."

"Well, men can get babies even when they're seventy and women stop when they're like thirty or something. That's what Garrett told me."

"Garrett, Garrett, everything Garrett. He doesn't know everything-"

"Okay, guys, I'm dying here. Can you move so I can get this stuff into the kitchen?" Ellie lifted her aching arm so she could give Simone a gentle nudge. Discussions about male and female fertility were all well and good but not when her siblings were standing there, blocking her path while they jabbered away, making her suffer with her load longer than was necessary.

"Sorry, Sis." Before she could stop him, Peter grabbed a second bag from her grasp and, heavy though it was, he swung it back and forth as he headed across the living room and toward the kitchen.

Ellie sighed in relief then followed him into the kitchen where she plopped the bag with milk, juice and eggs onto the table. "Where's Mom?" she asked as she glanced around.

"She's changing Kevin." Simone dropped Ellie's purse on top of the table, next to the bags. "He was playing with his trucks and then he got all stinky." She grimaced. "I am so glad I'm not a mom. Changing diapers is like the worst job ever."

Ellie smiled. "I know what you mean but Kevin's not even two yet. He can't help it." She picked up her purse. "I'll go check on them. Put the stuff away till I get back, okay?"

Peter groaned. "Do I have to?"

"Yes, you have to. I carried those bags all the way from Kingsbridge Road without a complaint. The least you can do is help me put them away." She spied Simone trying to sneak away. "Both of you."

"Aaw." Simone froze mid-step then turned, looking peeved. "Why can't Peter do it?"

"Because you're both good kids who love their big sister and don't want her to pass out from exhaustion. Right?" When there was no answer she put a hand on her hip but she was grinning. "Right, guys?"

"All right," Simone said grudgingly.

"Yeah, I guess," was Peter's grumbled response.

Ellie only laughed as she headed toward her mother's room. Typical kids. If they could get away without lifting a finger in the house that would suit them just fine. The only finger they had any interest in lifting was the one that moved the toggle on their Xbox.

"I'm here, Mom," she called out as she shrugged her business jacket off her shoulders. She'd dressed to impress for her interview but now that she was home she was just dying to get out of such formal wear. Besides, it had made her pretty hot during her walk from the supermarket.

"Hi, Ellie," her mom called back. "I'm in here with Kevin."

By this time Ellie was at the door, just in time to bend and open her arms as her little brother dashed toward her. The toddler squealed as she gathered him up into her arms and nuzzled his neck. "Mmm, you smell so good, little man."

"Ellie, Ellie," he chortled as he patted her face with his soft hands. "Ellie home."

"Yes, I'm home and ready to play with my favorite baby. Who's the best baby in the whole wide world?"

"Kevin!" He yelled his name and bounced up and down in Ellie's arms, obviously pleased with her praise.

Smiling, Abigail came forward and took Kevin from Ellie's arms. "You must be tired. You said you were going to stop at the grocery store."

"I did," Ellie replied and she shook her arms to get the blood pumping in them again. "That's why I got home so late but we're good for another week." She grinned. "Until I get my next pay check."

Abby shook her head then she sighed. "You're a good girl, Ellie. I don't know how we would have survived without you." Then her face grew more solemn. "I just wish you didn't have to drop out of university to help us."

"Mom, will you stop?" Ellie let out a hiss of frustration. They'd been over this a hundred times. "I would do anything for my family. I love you."

"And therein lies the problem..." Abby's words trailed off and her eyes took on a faraway look. "You've sacrificed your life for us."

"And you would have done the same if it had been your decision to make," Ellie retorted.

"But these are my children, Ellie, not yours. You have your whole life ahead of you."

"But they're my family. I love them more than anything." Suddenly overcome with emotion, Ellie put her arm around her mother's shoulders. "How could anyone have known that Frank would have died in a freak accident? It threw your world upside down. I couldn't let you deal with that alone."

"But I didn't want you to sacrifice your life for us." As she spoke, Abby's eyes glistened with unshed tears.

"It's okay, Mom. Universities will always be there but the kids need us. Right now. I can't let them down."

Kevin had begun to struggle in Abby's arms, clearly bored with the adult conversation, so she bent and lowered him to the ground. As soon as his feet touched the floor he took off toward the living room, back to his playthings. As Abby straightened, she shook her head. "There you go again, talking like you're the mom here. Always so responsible." She gave her daughter a look of bemusement. "You're so different from your father."

Ellie knew exactly what her mother meant. After struggling with her wayward husband until Ellie was seven, Abby had finally divorced him. She'd played the role of single mother for three years until she'd met Frank Esposito, an American who'd come to manage the hotel in the Cayman Islands where Abby worked. Within less than a year they'd fallen in love. They had a simple wedding then Frank took his new wife and eleven-year-old Ellie back to the United States where they lived happily as a family. When the first baby came when Ellie was thirteen she was over the moon. Two years later she got a baby sister and then, to the surprise of everyone, her mother got pregnant again at the age of forty-four.

Ellie had watched with tears in her eyes as Frank stood by his wife's hospital bed and held his son high, his eyes sparkling with pride. He was all of fifty-one years old but he was a daddy all over again and his love for his family shone bright in his eyes.

But their happiness was not to last. One winter night, on his way home, the slick and icy road made him lose control of the car. That was what the police told Abby when they showed up at the family home on that fateful evening. Frank's car had burst through the barrier and rolled over twice before landing, upside down, at the bottom of a steep ditch. He hadn't had a chance. Emergency vehicles were on the scene within minutes but by the time the paramedics got to him he'd drowned in the pool of water that had settled in the ditch. The only consolation the police could give was that he'd probably been totally unaware while he was drowning since the huge bump on his head was an indication that he'd been knocked unconscious.

When it happened, little Kevin had only been thirteen months old. Frank had died, leaving behind a very young family and a wife who was still so in love with him that she could not imagine life without him there. Abigail was devastated.

And then the trauma of Frank's sudden death was followed by an aftershock. Unbeknownst to Abby, Frank had let his life insurance policy lapse. Maybe it was because of all the traveling he'd been doing lately. Maybe he'd been too distracted. Whatever the reason, when it came time to renew the insurance policy it hadn't been done...for the first time in eleven years, at the worst possible time.

After the funeral, Ellie made a decision that she knew would have an impact on the rest of her life. It didn't matter, though. She knew what she had to do and she did not hesitate. Despite her mother's pleas, she withdrew from medical school and focused her attention on finding a job that would cover the expenses of a home on Long Island. With five mouths to feed, a mortgage and high property taxes, the pay scales of the jobs for which Ellie interviewed were woefully inadequate. And so, although at the time she'd turned him down, Ellie decided to contact the agent who had approached her on the university campus and given her his card. It was a good thing she hadn't thrown it out. She called Jeremy Fisher at Lord Modeling Agency. To her relief, even though it was four months later, he was still interested. She got the job.

It was this job that had kept the family going during the nine months since they'd lost Frank. They had to give up the house on Long Island and move to a smaller, more affordable home. Still, a three-bedroom apartment in the Bronx wasn't too bad as the children never went to bed hungry. Not even once. Ellie had been able to provide for all their needs and of that, she was immensely proud.

Until now...

At the thought of the new challenge that had surfaced, she sighed.

"Are you okay?" Abby tilted her head to one side as she gave her daughter a questioning look.

"I'm okay," she replied, but she knew her tone wasn't very convincing. Wanting to reassure her mother, she mustered a tiny smile. "I'm fine, Mom. I was just thinking about the situation with Peter. We can't let him continue like this."

Abby drew in her breath and now it was her turn to sigh. "I know you want to help but you can't do everything. You're already doing so much."

Ellie shook her head. "Not enough. I have to find a way..."

"Stop it, Ellie. You're already taking on too much. I told you, medication can help."

"I don't want that. I only want the best for my brother." She gazed off, past her mother's shoulder. "I've got to find a way to make more money."

. . ⌘ . .

"HE WAS ALWAYS A CANTANKEROUS old goat." Amadeo grumbled into his beer as he glared at Julio. His cousin knew how their grandfather's decisions irritated him sometimes but he was always bringing up the old man for discussion at the oddest moments.

Julio laughed, his dark eyes sparkling with mirth. "Well, he's even more cantankerous now that he's ninety."

Amadeo gave a grunt. "If you've lived that long I guess you can be a grumpy old *cabra* if you want to." It was a grudging comment but, if Amadeo should admit it to himself, he had a lot of respect for the old man who had worked his way up from fruit picker on a farm until he owned that same farm and all those surrounding it. He hadn't stopped until his worth had moved from a few pesos to millions of United States dollars. He'd tried to instill that same ambition and work ethic in all five of his children. The good news was that four of them had followed his example. The bad news was that one of them, addicted to gambling, had made wads of money then squandered it all. Amadeo had the misfortune of calling that one, Esteban, Papa.

At the thought of his father and the shame he had brought to the Castillo family, Amadeo shook his head as he tried to dispel the thoughts that always left him with a bitter taste on the tongue. As if being a compulsive gambler had not been bad enough, after Amadeo's mother died from cancer when he was only eleven years old, his father had proceeded to work his way through all of his possessions, selling everything in sight in order to finance his obsessive gambling habit. For the most part he had ignored his adolescent son, his only child, leaving him to fend for himself, sometimes abandoning him for days and weeks as he went on impromptu trips to Las Vegas, the casino capital of the world. It was while his father was away on a particularly long gambling trip that the neighbors reported the strange observation of a child putting out the garbage by himself, collecting the mail and keeping the flower garden from withering away due to lack of care. One of those same inquisitive neighbors had peeped in at the kitchen window while Amadeo had been busy fixing dinner. He'd quickly pulled the curtains closed but it was too late. By the next day the police were knocking at the door, demanding to speak with the head of the household. No amount of bluffing on Amadeo's part could get rid of them and so, by the time Esteban got back, his son had been transplanted. He now lived with Esteban's father, *Senor* Rodrigo Castillo. He was now the ward of one of the wealthiest men in all of Argentina.

But that did not mean Amadeo had an easy life. *Abuelo* Castillo was a strict, no-nonsense man who demanded perfection, even from an eleven-year-old. Amadeo learned early that, for Rodrigo Castillo, only the best was good enough.

"So how's the old man doing?" Although he didn't say it out loud, he had a soft spot for the man who had taken him from adolescence into adulthood, teaching him invaluable lessons about business and work ethics. It didn't matter that Rodrigo had wasted little time on any show of affection toward the boy. It was as if all he knew was how to be firm. Ruthless, even. And that was what he had taught his grandson - how to be tough. "Has he gotten over the cramping in his hands?"

Julio shook his head. "No, he won't get over that too easily. It's arthritis. It's a wonder that, at his age, that's his only ailment. If you ask me, I'd say he's a darned lucky son-of-a-gun."

"Son of a gun..." Amadeo repeated the words, letting them trail off as he spared Julio a slight smile. His cousin, who had gone to high school in Florida, sounded more American than all his relatives. Only two years younger than Amadeo's thirty-two, he had a youthful look and a cosmopolitan air that made him seem much younger. "I don't know if Rodrigo would appreciate being described as such."

"Yeah, well I wouldn't call him that to his face. I was never one to disrespect my elders." Julio grinned.

"Not to mention, our grandfather would not hesitate to reprimand you for that." Amadeo grimaced at the thought. Rodrigo was never one to hold his sharp tongue. He took another sip of his beer then cocked an eyebrow in Julio's direction. "So what's this I hear about you going back to school?"

Julio nodded, looking proud of himself. "Yup. I'll be doing my M.B.A at Duke University. They have a good business program."

Amadeo gave a snort. "It's hard to picture you back in school."

"And why is it so hard to believe?"

"It's just not the Julio I know." Amadeo couldn't hold back his grin. "As long as you stay focused on your studies and don't get distracted by the ladies, all will be well."

Julio didn't respond to that one. He just gave Amadeo a sly look, which meant he had something up his sleeve. His silence meant he wasn't ready to show his hand.

Amadeo didn't bother to press. He just shook his head. "Tell you what, when you're at school you might want to try my philosophy – use them then lose them. It's always worked for me. Reduces complications."

Julio gave him a skeptical look. "It sounds like a sure way to get your face slapped."

"Don't knock it till you've tried it." But even as the words left Amadeo's mouth, his mind was wandering back to a moment earlier that day when he'd stared into the dark eyes of a woman whose gaze was so defiant, yet so haunting, that he could not get it out of his mind.

A sure way to get your face slapped, Julio said. And if ever there was a woman who would dare to make that move, Amadeo knew that Ellie Goldwell would be the one.

He only hoped she never tried it. He would hate to have to put his newly-appointed spokesmodel in her place. And then, at the thought, his lips softened in a private smile. Having to punish little Miss Priss might not be such a bad thing. He might actually enjoy it.

But the titillating thought did not make him forget why he never let his relationships go too deep. As far as he was knew, where desirable women were concerned, the best thing to do was to never get your heart involved with them...especially hauntingly beautiful ones like Ellie Goldwell.

CHAPTER THREE

On Wednesday morning when Ellie showed up at the photo studio of Aura Cosmetics she found a very different Jack Usher running the show. The quiet, reserved man she'd met the day before had been replaced by a focused, forceful dictator who barked orders like he was leader of his own private army. Today, directing the photo shoot, Jack Usher was in his element.

As soon as she walked through the door he whisked her off and plopped her down in front of the make-up artist. "Get her ready," he ordered. "We don't have a minute to spare." And then he was off, shouting commands to his team and giving clipped responses to their requests. It was obvious that, when the occasion called for it, he was all business.

"Esther, what are you doing over there?" He latched onto a young woman who was standing in the shadows, staring over at Ellie as she sat perched on a stool while the make-up artist studied her face. "You're supposed to be sorting outfits. Now get to it."

Esther, tall and gangly and a good six inches taller than Jack, looked like she was used to his new, domineering attitude because she simply shrugged and turned away. "I was just checking out our new model," she said, her tone casual and with just a hint of amusement. She pushed her black-framed glasses up her nose. "Everything will go smoothly, Jack, just like it always does. No need to get all flustered."

"I am not flustered. I simply want everything to be perfect. Perfect!" The last word was practically a shout, making Esther lift her eyebrows. If she hadn't gotten the message before, she certainly got it now. Jack Usher meant business.

Esther scurried back to her post just as a red-haired man walked in the door, a camera around his neck and two more hanging from his shoulder. "Hey, Jack," he called out as he walked across the room. "You guys ready for me?"

"Ready for you? You're over thirty minutes late. You should have set up already." Jack was clearly not amused.

"Yeah, but Simone needs time to do her thing. Why would I come set up and then have to wait an hour while the model's face gets fixed? Right, Simone?"

"Brandon Carter, you leave me out of this." The make-up artist was chuckling as she gently stroked the brush over Ellie's cheek. "I'm busy doing my work. If you know what's good for you, you'd better go do yours."

"Yes, Brandon. Time waits for no man. Before you know it, it will be the end of the day and if we don't get the photos we need for the launch of the new cosmetics line we'll be up the creek." Jack fixed his glare on the photographer. "And you don't want Amadeo Castillo coming in here, only to find out that we haven't accomplished our task."

At the sound of Amadeo's name Brandon's smug look disappeared and he frowned. "No, we don't want that happening, do we?" He mumbled the words but Ellie heard every one of them.

She knew exactly how Brandon Carter felt. She'd been in a good mood, amused by the banter between the crew and Jack, but when the name of the company's owner left Jack's lips her mood took a dramatic turn...for the worse. It was like that name, Amadeo Castillo, threw cold water over everything.

Simone cleared her throat and turned away, suddenly looking super-busy as she sorted through jars and tubes of foundation. Esther headed over to the racks of clothing and began going through the outfits as if trying to find a specific one. Brandon went over to the wall where the backdrop had already been set up and began pulling stands forward so he could arrange his cameras. Jack, though, was looking pleased. He could see that he'd played his cards right. Just the mention of Amadeo's name had his workers becoming focused and serious.

And Ellie, although not part of Jack's team, was no less affected. To her chagrin, at the mention of Amadeo's name her heart did a backflip in her chest, making her aware that she was just as scared of the man as his employees were. Maybe scared was too strong a word but the thought of Amadeo definitely had an impact and not a good one, either.

As she sat still, awaiting Simone's next round of beauty applications, her thoughts went back to the rigid face of the man who, for the next week or two, would be her client. As a representative of Lord Modeling Agency it was her responsibility to make the client happy. That was not going to be an easy task. She'd already met the man and, from only one meeting, she could tell he was demanding, exacting and unforgiving. The reactions she'd observed just now were further proof that he was a hard man to deal with. When it came to his high standards and demands she only hoped she could deliver.

After that jarring reminder of the man who paid the bills, everyone got super-focused and Ellie was soon made up and ready for the camera. Esther ushered her over to the dressing room where she carefully draped colorful scarves over the elegant black gown she'd selected for their model. She then walked her back to the set where Brandon would position her and set the lights so they would illuminate her in the best possible way. Jack, as usual, was hovering around like a mother hen, making sure everything was just right.

"I don't like that light, Brandon. Too yellow. It makes her look like she's glowing." He was tut-tutting as he shook his head.

"But that's a good thing, isn't it? A slight glow makes her look healthy."

"Or like a fairy. We're not shooting Tinker Bell. We're shooting the woman who will represent Aura Cosmetics for the next year. Now change it."

Brandon frowned. "I'm the photographer here-"

"Change it." Jack folded his arms across his chest and stood glaring at the photographer until, with a resigned sigh, the young man moved to do as he'd been ordered.

After that, things settled down and the day went smoothly. From time to time Brandon would call to Simone to freshen up the face powder as the heat from the powerful lights drew a dewy film onto Ellie's brows. He would then get back to photographing, snapping away, capturing so many images that she wondered when he would ever find the time to go through all of them.

They'd been at it for over four hours when Jack, their slave driver for the day, finally put up his hand. "Good job, guys. You deserve a break."

Simone dabbed at her brow. "Well, finally. I was about to pass out from the heat." She stepped back and away from the spotlight that had been trained on Ellie all morning. She'd been freshening the make-up again and again, and each time she'd done that she'd had to share the heat of the lights with Ellie. For Simone, those random minutes under the lights were enough.

An exhausted sigh escaped Ellie's lips. After four hours of constant heat and glare, she was wilting. The whole time she'd been baking under the lights she'd had to forgo refreshments, even water. Simone didn't want her to mess up the exquisite job she'd done with the make-up. Simone's words, not Ellie's.

And so she'd suffered through it, parched and perspiring but not complaining, just wanting to get the day and the job done. She was tiring, though, and when Jack called for the break it was not a moment too soon.

Ellie was sliding off the padded stool on which she'd been perched when, all of a sudden, the room went silent. Jack's animated chatter, Esther's murmurs and Brandon's snickers, they all stopped as if someone had flipped the off switch. She turned just in time to see a man, tall and dark in navy blue business suit, enter the room. Amadeo Castillo.

"Finished?" It was one word, but said so imperiously that everyone's brows shot up.

Jack stepped forward. "We've been hard at it since this morning," he said. "We still have a long way to go but I decided it was time for a break."

Amadeo's brows fell. "It is after two o'clock. Before you know it, it will be time for these people to head for home. Are you at least halfway through?"

"No. I...we still have the lounge photos and the outdoor photos to do. We will get through it all. I promise." Jack threw a glance at Brandon as if seeking support to execute that promise, and then he looked back at his boss. "They will be quick in refreshing themselves and then they'll be back on the job."

"Good. There is no time for slacking off. We are on a deadline and I expect-"

"No, you did not just say that." The words flew past Ellie's lips before she could clamp her mouth shut. "You're not calling us slackers, are you? You couldn't be." After they'd been working so hard, the audacity of the man to pass judgment. She wouldn't stand for it.

Amadeo swung around, seeming to notice her for the first time, and the look he gave her was one of incredulity. "You dare to question my authority?"

"I'm not questioning your authority. I'm simply defending a team of hardworking people who just spent the last four hours working like dogs so you could have the photos for your product launch. We've been going non-stop without a single break, and you just march in and make it seem like we've been twiddling our thumbs." Ellie knew she was treading on very dangerous ground. In fact, from the look on Amadeo's face she could tell she'd done the unthinkable – she'd talked back to the big boss. From the grim look on his face it was quite clear that he was not used to such a response.

She stole a quick glance at Jack then at Brandon and they were both staring at her like she'd gone mad. And if she didn't know it before, the shock on their faces was all she needed to see, to understand the mess she was in.

She glanced back at Amadeo and his jaw had gone rigid, his anger obvious in the throbbing pulse at the base of his throat. Knowing she'd put her foot in it, she thought fast. Somehow, she had to make him understand. "We haven't had a break all morning," she began to explain. "We deserve-"

"That's enough. I will see you in my office. Five minutes. Do not be late." His stare was cold and hard, reserved only for her. He didn't look at anyone else in the room. And then as she gazed up at him, wondering why she couldn't have held her tongue, he turned and stalked out of the room, leaving her staring after him.

As soon as Amadeo was out of earshot Jack turned to her. "Are you mad? Don't you know who that is?"

"I know." This time Ellie's voice was quiet. She felt like all her strength had just been sucked out of her.

"That was Amadeo Castillo, the owner of the company," Jack continued as if she hadn't just answered him. "Why would you question him like that? You just defied him." He said the words like he still couldn't believe it.

"I didn't...mean to. It was just...I just couldn't stand it, the way he barged in and started speaking down to us like we're worth nothing." She shook her head. Was it so bad, standing up for yourself, even if it meant upsetting the man who paid their wages?

Simone and Esther exchanged glances and a tiny smile began to curve Esther's lips. It was fleeting but still, it was a small indication that they approved of what she'd done. They would not judge her and that meant a lot.

Brandon chuckled, drawing Ellie's attention to his smiling face. "You go, girl. Owner or not, I guess he'll think twice before stepping on your toes. You're a wolf in sheep's clothing. I never knew we had a fighter in our midst."

Jack didn't look quite so impressed. "You'd better get going if you know what's good for you. He said five minutes."

She nodded. "Okay, I'm going." At least three out of the five minutes had already passed but it didn't matter. She was already in it deep so what was one more transgression?

But then her throat constricted and her heart tightened in her chest, forcing her to admit her trepidation. She'd pissed off the most powerful man she'd ever met, one who could make or break her. And the million-dollar question was, how in the world was she going to appease him?

. . ✿ . .

MIERDA. The girl had some nerve speaking to him like that. And worse, in front of his employees.

Amadeo mumbled under his breath as he paced the floor. He glanced at the clock above the door. One minute. Ellie Goldwell had one minute before he went right back down there and fired her on the spot. If she didn't make it by the time-

A quick tap and the door opened, bringing his racing thoughts to a screeching halt. A head popped in. It was Claudia.

"Excuse me, sir," his secretary said as she threw him an apologetic look. "I don't see her on your schedule but Miss

Ellie Goldwell is here to see you. She said you are expecting her."

"Yes." Amadeo gave her a curt nod. "Send her in."

Her face serious as usual, the woman gave him an equally curt nod then turned to the person standing behind her. "You may go in, Miss Goldwell. Mr. Castillo will see you now."

Claudia stepped aside and, looking too calm and collected to suit Amadeo, Ellie walked in. He'd expected hesitation, maybe even a little bit of fear. But this? The girl had a haughty air about her that made it seem like he'd called her up to his office for a diplomatic discussion rather than a resounding reprimand. He would definitely have to take her down a notch or two.

Amadeo stepped back and, folding his arms across his chest, he watched as she entered the room then glanced at him, her eyes guarded and her lips tight. He jerked his head toward the chair that faced his desk. "Have a seat." He didn't wait for her to comply. He walked on ahead of her, straight to the bay windows, where he clasped his hands behind his back as he stared down at the busy streets of Manhattan.

He waited until he heard her take her seat and then he began. "Your behavior downstairs was unacceptable. I do not expect my authority to be questioned. Do not let this happen again."

For a moment there was silence and he almost turned to see why she did not answer but then she spoke, and when she did her voice was quiet but firm.

"I did not mean to be rude," she said, "but you were being unreasonable. I could not let you speak to us like that."

"You could not?" He swung around to glare at her. "I pay good money for your services. The least you could have done was hold your tongue." And then he glanced up and saw that his office door was ajar. "You did not close the door behind you?"

She lifted her face and glared right back. "You were standing there when I walked in."

She was right. He should have been the one to close it. With the door open, Claudia must have heard quite an earful. Angry with himself, he marched over and closed it with a firm click then turned back to face the cause of his ire. He strode over to where she sat, her back rigid, her eyes flashing, her chin tilted upward as if she intended to face him head on. He wasn't used to such a show of defiance. She was a brave one. He would give her that much.

He stood there, staring down at her until a pink blush crept up her neck and colored her cheeks. He bit back a smile. So the ice princess was capable of being embarrassed. Good.

He walked over to the desk and sat down in his high-backed leather chair then swiveled around to face her. "Miss Goldwell," he said, his voice deliberately cool, "let me make myself clear. As long as you work for me you will show respect for my authority. You will not speak to me like that, ever again."

There was a sudden intake of breath and her eyes widened. "But I don't work for-" Then, as if she'd been struck by a sudden thought, she bit down on her bottom lip and dropped her gaze.

This time Amadeo could not hold back a sardonic smile. It had sunk in at last. He could see it on her face. Ellie Goldwell was finally understanding that he was the one holding the handle while she held the blade.

Satisfied, he picked up the gold pen lying on his desk and began to scribble on his notepad. "You may go now," he said, and he did not bother to look up.

Ellie did not say another word. He heard her rise. There was the tap of her stilettos as she crossed the hardwood floor. The door opened and then it closed quietly behind her. She was gone.

It was only then that he looked up but as he stared at the deep, dark brown of the mahogany door he frowned. He'd won the battle this time but if he'd read Ellie Goldwell right, there would be more battles to come. The real question was, which one of them would win the war.

CHAPTER FOUR

"But I never said anything like that. Honest." Ellie's heart thumped in her chest as she clutched her cell phone to her ear. She'd just left the photo shoot and, exhausted, was climbing into her car when the phone rang. "I spoke up for myself, I'll admit that, but I wasn't rude to him. I swear."

"Well, that's not what I heard," Jeremy Fisher grated into the phone. "What the hell got into you? Don't you know you could have cost us this contract? Heck, we could have lost it already. Who knows if the man won't pick up the phone and tell me to forget it?"

"B...but I don't see how this could-"

"You don't see how? Because of what you did the man may never use our modeling agency again." He sounded like, if she'd been nearby, he would have wrung her neck. "You could have already cost us thousands."

Ellie swallowed. "I'm...sorry. I didn't think-"

"You're damn right, you didn't. You really messed this up. You know that, don't you?" He paused, waiting for her answer.

Ellie could not speak. It took a full four seconds before she could utter another word. When she finally did, her voice was little more than a choked whisper. "Did Amadeo...Mr. Castillo...tell you that? That I swore at him and called him a jerk?"

"He didn't have to. I got it from a reliable source."

Ellie gritted her teeth. Claudia. It had to be. Somehow she couldn't see Esther, Simone or Brandon ratting on her like that. Not even Jack. And then to add all those embellishments, that she'd sworn at Amadeo and called him names? Someone was intent on getting her fired and the only person she could think of was that secretary of his. She must have overheard the conversation. Either that, or she'd heard something through the office grapevine and then added her own spin to it. The witch.

"Don't believe any of it, Jeremy. Mr. Castillo and I had a discussion. We came to an understanding."

The agent gave a snort that reflected his disgust. "D'you know what? I don't even want to hear it. You just make sure that, from here on, Mr. Castillo is one hundred percent satisfied with you in every possible way," he paused as if for effect, "or else you're out." He didn't wait for her reply. The sudden click told Ellie the conversation was over, whether she liked it or not.

Her chest still tight, she released her breath and slumped against the car, suddenly realizing how much trouble she was in...and at the worst possible time. She'd tripped and tumbled into a nightmare just when she needed to protect her income at all costs, just when she'd been racking her brain to find ways to earn more. Her family was depending on her. How could she have been so foolish?

Her mother would always warn her about her sharp tongue, that it would get her into a real pickle one day. Well, that day had come and the worst thing about it was, she couldn't say a word to Abby. She couldn't bear to see the disappointment on her mother's face if she told her how she'd jeopardized the welfare of the whole family just to make a point.

And so, when she got home that evening, she clamped her lips shut and said not a word. When her mother commented on how quiet she was she simply shrugged and told her she was tired. And then she went to bed early but only to lie there, staring up at the ceiling, wishing she could tell Amadeo Castillo what she really thought about him – that he was an arrogant, self-centered bully who thought money gave him license to talk down to people – but, of course, she couldn't. Not as long as she worked for an agency that, in essence, worked for him. As the futility of her situation sank in Ellie drew in a long breath then let it out in a frustrated sigh. Where Amadeo Castillo was concerned, she could only pray that whatever was left of her contract with his corporation would be short and uneventful. She could hardly wait to see the back of that terrible man.

But as she drifted off to sleep that night, the last thing she remembered was those deep gray eyes that Amadeo had fixed on her and those lips, so firm, so strong. With his demeanor, so assertive, even aggressive, he was obviously not short on testosterone. Amadeo Castillo was all man.

And the last conscious thought Ellie had was that, contrary though it may be, she was curious to know what it would be like to be kissed by such a man.

. . ❧ . .

AMADEO FELT DISTURBED. Something was not right.

This was the second day of the photo shoot and, like he'd done the day before, he'd gone down to the studio to check how much progress his team had made. They had a deadline to meet and they were going to make that date, no matter what. He had no time for foul-ups or excuses.

He'd entered the studio, his eyes immediately scanning the room in search of Ellie, expecting her to respond with a glare or some other show of defiance. In a second he found her, as poised and elegant as she'd been the day before, but when she saw him her eyes widened and then she dropped her gaze. Even as he greeted the team he was staring at her, for a full nine or ten seconds, but she never looked up, not even when he said her name. Head still down, she simply responded with a quiet, almost inaudible whisper, "Good afternoon, Mr. Castillo."

What the *diablos*? Had he cowed the girl that much? This was not the Ellie who, like a queen, had haughtily strutted out of his office the day before. Could she have heard he'd spoken to her boss at the agency?

And then she lifted her head and he saw it – the flash of rebellion in her eyes that told him she was just as feisty as ever. For some strange reason, she'd wanted him to think otherwise. The girl was a devious one. He could see that now. She might not know it but he was not an easy man to fool.

She probably hated every moment he was there but he spent over half an hour...deliberately...observing as the photographer gave his model instructions on how to pose for the various shots. As he watched, he discussed the upcoming campaign with Jack.

"We want this to have an international flair," he told his creative director. "Cosmeticos Aurora is all about style, class. What do you think about that gown she's wearing? Conservative, don't you think?"

Jack didn't answer right away. He was staring at Ellie and there was hint of a smile on his lips. He shook his head. "Not at all," he said, his tone surprisingly confident, even smug. "Ellie is all class. She can wear anything and make it look just right. And the make-up." He shook his head. "Perfect. She represents us well."

Amadeo swung his eyes back to Ellie. With that, he had to agree. There were few models who had walked through these doors who had captured the essence of Aura Cosmetics so well. Ellie was one of them.

But, as happy as he was with how well she was handling the job, it was time to move on to phase two of his plan to take full control; time to make her understand, without a doubt, that he was boss.

He strode across the studio and came to a stop directly in front of her. It didn't matter that the photographer was aiming the camera lens at her, getting ready to take another shot. He'd spent enough time in the studio and now it was time to give Ellie her instructions so he could head back to his office and his work.

"As soon as the photo shoot ends you will come to see me," he told her. "Do not keep me waiting." He did not wait for her response. He turned and strode away and, as he did, he could feel five pairs of eyes boring into his back.

He'd been called an arrogant brute before. He'd also been called worse. He knew he lived up to all those titles and more, but he did not care. When you were the owner of a multi-billion dollar corporation you did what you had to do. Making friends was not a top priority on that list of things to do.

It was not until almost six o'clock that evening that he heard the tap on the door that signaled Ellie's arrival. "Come in." This time, when he gave the permission to enter, it was not a head of sleek black hair that he saw, since Claudia had already left for home. It was Ellie's dark auburn hair that appeared and this time it was pulled back in a sleek French roll that gave even greater emphasis to her high cheekbones and expressive dark eyes. But now, to his annoyance, the expression in those eyes was unreadable.

As she pushed the door open and entered the room, his brows fell. "This is late," he said, his tone curt.

"But I'm not," she shot back. "You said to come right after the photo shoot. It just ended."

Amadeo would have smiled if he hadn't made up his mind to be ultra-firm with this girl. This was more like it. The spirited Ellie Goldwell was back. "I will take your word for it," he said, his voice deliberately cool. "Now have a seat so we can talk."

She raised her eyebrows, obviously curious about what he had to say, but she did not stop to question him. She did as he'd ordered, crossing the room to take the seat across from him. Then, adopting a deceptively meek attitude, she folded her hands in her lap.

He was not fooled. Under that placid surface were raging rapids that Ellie was doing her best to hide. It was too late. He'd known her for just a couple of days but already he could read the storm that raged behind those onyx eyes. She must have spoken to her boss at Lord Modeling Agency and that was why she was playing super-cool. She knew why he'd called her here. She must know, at this point, that it was best not to step on his toes.

He didn't bother to mince words. "So he told you. You know why you're here?"

Ellie's eyes widened. Looking like she had no idea what he was talking about, she gave him a questioning look. "Who told me? Told me what?"

Amadeo narrowed his gaze as he stared back at her. He could tell that she knew, so why was she playing ignorant? "Jeremy Fisher. Did you not have a conversation with him?"

"Y...ye-e-es." She stretched the word out like she was unsure, then gave him a look of uncertainty.

"Then he should have told you that, effective today, you are no longer employed to Lord Modeling Agency."

Like she'd just received the shock of her life, Ellie jerked upright in the chair, eyes wide and jaw slack. When she opened her mouth it was to gasp her words out. "Wh...what did you say?"

Amadeo scowled. What kind of game was she playing? "You said you spoke to Jeremy. You discussed all this."

"No," she whispered, her voice full of distress. "He said nothing. I...don't believe this. I've been fired?"

Amadeo gave a snort of derision. "I wouldn't call it that. It's more like a change of status."

At his words, the expression on Ellie's face changed. Now, instead of distress, all he could read was confusion. "What do you mean?"

That made him pause. "What, exactly, did you discuss with Jeremy today?"

She shook her head. "I didn't speak with him today. Our conversation was yesterday."

It was only when she said that, that Amadeo realized she had no idea why she was in his office. He nodded. "So, you are in the dark. Your agency has been tardy in their communication with you." He fixed his gaze on her flushed face. "I bought your twelve month contract. As of today you answer to me and me alone."

Ellie's brows jerked up, surprise again registered on her face. Then, realizing she was still employed, her face relaxed and she sagged back into her chair. Her relief was fleeting. Within seconds the confusion was back and with it, a hint of fear. "But...why?" She was frowning now, gripping the arms of her chair as if for support.

He would give her an explanation, he decided. That was only fair. "The outcome of this campaign will have significant impact on my business. Nobody controls my business. Nobody but me."

He got up from his chair and walked over to the window, his back to her. He'd never been able to sit still for too long. As a child he'd been punished often enough for not being able to stay still. He had to resist the urge to start pacing.

When he turned back to face Ellie she was watching him, waiting. He wondered if she understood what he was saying. "I control everything about this project, Ellie. Including you."

She swallowed but still, she said nothing. He admired that, a woman who was capable of holding her tongue.

"Do you have a passport?"

The question made her raise her brows again. "Yes. Why?"

"Tomorrow you will speak with my secretary. She will give you information and get the relevant travel documents from you. Next Monday you will leave for Argentina."

For the second time that evening Ellie sucked in her breath on a gasp. "Argentina? I...I have to travel?"

She was annoying him now. "This is an international company," he said, not hiding his impatience. "Of course you will have to travel."

"The agency never told me this job would require travel."

"You work for me now. What they may or may not have told you is irrelevant. You answer only to me."

At his words, a flash of panic lit up Ellie's eyes. It looked like the girl was finally beginning to understand. If she wanted to stay employed she would have to be far more compliant than she'd been earlier. And she would have to learn to hold her tongue. Apparently, this realization was just beginning to sink in.

Satisfied that he'd made her new position clear, Amadeo decided to bring their meeting to an end. He walked past her then opened the office door. "Thank you for coming. If you have any questions you may speak with my secretary tomorrow."

Ellie got up but her movement was slow, as if she were stunned. She walked toward him, her brows slightly furrowed, and as she got to the door she paused and looked up at him. "Thank you, Mr. Castillo," she said and her eyes were so full of doubt that he could tell that her thoughts were a thousand miles away. Obviously, she had a lot on her mind.

But that wasn't his problem.

And then she spoke again. "Do I need to go so far away?"

Amadeo stared down at her, not responding right away. She was hesitating about a trip that most women her age would leap at. That could only mean one thing. There must be a man in her life, one that she could not bear to leave behind even if her purpose for going was to work.

And then he caught himself. What the devil did that have to do with him? She could have a million men if she wanted. It was none of his business. Annoyed at himself, he frowned. When her brows lifted, he realized she must think he was frowning at her. He drew in his breath in an effort to relax. What he got was a breath of the flowery fragrance of her perfume. "I need you in Argentina next week," he said. "Is that a problem?"

"Yes." She blurted the word out and then she shook her head. "No. I mean..." She drew in her breath. "Do I have to do this now?"

Annoyed that she would question his plan, Amadeo shook his head. "No, you do not have to do this now. You do not have to do anything. No-one is irreplaceable, Ellie. It is your choice." He continued to stare down at her, awaiting her response.

For a swift second Ellie looked stricken and then she dropped her eyes, but not before he'd seen the flush that rose in her cheeks and the trembling of her lips. She swallowed then drew in a shallow breath. It made her seem so vulnerable that Amadeo's first instinct was to reach out and touch her.

He held back just in time. Annoyed at his reaction to the girl's show of distress, possibly because she would have to leave a lover behind, Amadeo hardened his gaze. "Your choice?" he asked, demanding her decision right then.

She lifted a hand and when she touched her fingers to her lips he saw that they were trembling. She swallowed again. "I will go." It was a soft whisper, almost inaudible, but it filled him with immense satisfaction.

This was battle number two and he had won. Ellie Goldwell had yielded to his will. It was a good way to start his working relationship with the woman who would soon become the face of his corporation. This was exactly the way he liked things and, if he continued to exercise his control, there would be no battle number three.

He had essentially won the war. Perfect.

CHAPTER FIVE

"This isn't happening to me. This is not happening." Ellie was whispering the words to herself, her heart tightening with every step she took toward her Toyota Corolla as it sat at the far end of the parking lot. By the time she got to her car she was so tightly wound she had to stop to suck in several deep breaths.

With one quick decision he'd made, Amadeo had brought a sledgehammer down on her world.

When she finally opened the car door and sank down onto the driver's seat her thoughts were still in a state of turmoil. She stared, unseeing, at the almost deserted parking lot that stretched before her. How would she break this to her mother? She would have to leave her family, she didn't even know for how long, right at the time when they needed her most.

Another four minutes passed before she sighed then turned the key in the ignition. There was nothing to be done but to tell Abby about this unfortunate turn of events. Together they would figure out the best way to deal with it.

But when she got home Ellie got a big surprise. Abby was not at all upset. "This is an excellent opportunity," she said on hearing the news. "An international assignment? This is your biggest one yet. You never know where this might take you."

For a moment Ellie could only stare at her mother in disbelief. "Mom, did you hear what I just said? I'm leaving next week for Argentina. Argentina, Mom!" The way she said it, her voice full of distressed incredulity, it was like she was talking about leaving for the moon. And it might as well have been. Argentina was thousands of miles away. "How can I go so far away, especially now?" She shook her head. "I don't want to go. Not now. Peter needs me."

Instead of agreeing with her daughter, Abby gave Ellie a look that was tinged with regret. "You've already done so much. You gave up medical school-"

"Mom, we've already talked about that, over and over again. Can we not go there? Please." She got up from the kitchen table and went over to plug in the hot pot. She could do with some tea to steady her jangling nerves. "Peter had another epileptic seizure just last week and the doctor said it will happen again, maybe soon. I don't want to be away from home, not until he's started treatment."

Abby swiveled around on her chair to look over at Ellie. "But even if you're here his treatment won't get started until we find the money. My part-time job won't do much, but the fact that you're going on an international assignment might mean that you'll make the kind of money you've been wanting to make, so you can help Peter. Did you think of that?"

Ellie frowned and turned around, forgetting her tea for the moment. "Do you really think that's what will happen? That I'll make more money?" Her heart thumped at the thought. Just the night before she'd tossed and turned, trying to figure out how she could handle the assignments for her modeling contract while taking on a part-time job. Could things turn out where she would be able to make enough money from this one modeling contract?

"I think it could happen. It would only make sense." Abby lifted an eyebrow. "Maybe you could speak to Mr. Fisher about it on Monday?" Then, as she saw Ellie's hesitation, she quickly added, "Or just leave it alone. I'm sure he'll broach the subject before you head out on your trip." When her daughter didn't respond she frowned. "Are you all right? You look a bit pale." She made as if to rise but Ellie put up a hand to stop her.

"There's something I have to tell you," she said, her voice subdued. She swallowed and when next she spoke she did not look her mother in the eyes. "I don't work for Lord Modeling Agency anymore. Mr. Castillo bought my contract. I work for him now." She'd said the last part in a rush, quickly clarifying that she still had a job. The last thing she wanted to do was scare her mother unnecessarily.

Abby's surprise was obvious. Her eyebrows shot up and she cocked her head to one side as she looked up at Ellie. "He did? I didn't even know you could do that, buy someone's work contract. Is that even possible?" There was a bemused expression on her face as she asked the question.

"Apparently, it is. From what he told me, it's a done deal." For a moment Ellie was silent as she thought about that. Even as she said it she didn't like the sound of it. It was like she hadn't had any choice in the matter. No, clearly, she hadn't. She'd been sold to the first available bidder, just like that. For all intents and purposes, she was now the possession of the most disagreeable man she'd ever met. She grimaced. "I guess that's why he practically ordered me to go to Argentina. I work for him now."

Abby looked thoughtful and then the slight furrows on her brow cleared. "Like I said, maybe things will work out in your favor. He may be generous-"

"I doubt it." Ellie's response was quick and it was dry. She knew the man. She could tell he was the type who wouldn't pay a cent over the rate stipulated in her contract. Abby was just being the optimist, as usual. She sighed. "But I guess I have to go. What else can I do? Right now it's the only way for me to get the money for Peter's treatment."

Abby's face turned serious and then she nodded. "You go on that trip and do the best darned job you can. Knock the socks off that man. Hey, he may love you so much he might even give you a bonus."

That made Ellie smile. "You're something else, Mom. Ever the dreamer."

Her mother drew in her breath then let it out on a sigh. "That's what keeps me going, honey. That's what keeps me sane." She gazed off toward the window, looking like her mind had wandered to a place far away, a distant place but a not so distant time. Ellie knew that, right at that moment, her mother's thoughts were on what her life used to be. With Frank.

Then she blinked. She shook her head and when she looked at Ellie again there was new determination in her eyes. "You do what you have to do in Argentina," she said. "While you're doing that I'll see if I can set up a meeting with the Neurofeedback Center."

"But why? Without health insurance you know we'll have to pay full price. It costs thousands. Right now we don't have that kind of money."

"No, but I bet they offer a payment plan. How many people would have that kind of money to pay up front?" Abby gave the table a smart pat with her palm. "If we have a payment plan in place things will work out. You're doing your part. Now it's time for me to do mine." She gave Ellie a confident smile. "Peter will get his neurofeedback therapy. Together we'll make it happen."

And with those words Ellie knew her fate was sealed. She was going to Argentina to earn as much as she could so she could cover the cost of Peter's treatment. She couldn't bear it if he had another epileptic seizure.

And if the cost of his healing was that she should spend her every waking moment with Amadeo Castillo, then so be it. She only hoped, with his arrogant self, he didn't drive her crazy in the process.

•• ❧ ••

"WHEN WILL YOU GET SERIOUS and settle down? You're not getting any younger." Rodrigo Castillo might be ninety years old but as he glared at Amadeo his eyes were as sharp as ever. "You're just like the others. All my grandsons are the same, sowing wild oats all over the place but not giving me any great-grandchildren." He shook his head and gave a hiss of annoyance. "I raised you from the age of eleven. I thought you would be different."

On arriving in Argentina, the first person Amadeo had decided to visit was his grandfather. Now he looked at Rodrigo askance. "Me? Rush into marriage and be the next victim of the Castillo curse? I don't think so."

Rodrigo's eyes narrowed but, for the moment at least, he fell silent. Amadeo could tell the old man's thoughts had flown back to the experience that had made him who he was – cold, demanding and unyielding, unwilling to show much emotion outside of anger, even to the grandson who had been in his care. No, especially to that grandson. Amadeo knew first-hand that his grandfather was not an easy man to live with. In old age he was as ruthless and deliberate as ever, especially where business was concerned.

But Amadeo knew something else about the old man. As hard as he might be, he had a loyalty to family that could not be denied. For him, the prosperity and growth of the Castillo clan was everything.

"Do not be swayed by my experiences," the old man said and as he sat forward in his chair, his grip tightening on his walking stick, he fixed his gray eyes on Amadeo. "My experiences made me bitter but my life is not yours. You have no excuse for not producing the next generation."

Amadeo gave him a bitter smile. Easy for the old man to say. "Why are you harassing us guys to start families? You've got granddaughters, too."

"That is true but their children will not carry the Castillo name. Before I die I want my grandsons to give me the next generation of Castillos."

Amadeo shook his head. "Don't look in my direction. I have no time for any woman looking for commitment. As far as I'm concerned, they're good for one thing and one thing only." He got up and went over to grip his grandfather's arm and steady him as he stood.

Independent as always, the old man shook his arm off then, with the aid of his walking stick, he crossed the room and headed over to the sideboard where he poured himself a glass of *Fernet* and topped it up with soda water. He took a sip of the herbal liqueur then turned back toward Amadeo. "Use them then lose them?" he asked, giving his grandson a pointed look.

Amadeo didn't bother to hide his disdain. "*Exactamente.*" Clingy, needy women, he could do without.

Rodrigo gave a grunt. "I used to think that way, too. I was a hard man."

Amadeo couldn't help the sardonic smile that crept onto his lips. Was? As far as he was concerned, his grandfather was as cold and hard as he'd ever been.

Rodrigo seemed not to notice. "I changed," he continued. "Life is too short to be so bitter."

At that point Amadeo had heard enough. He was in no mood for lectures and it sounded like Rodrigo was preparing to deliver one. He gave the older man a curt nod. "I'm sorry but I must go now," he said. "I have a meeting scheduled with the marketing department at the Buenos Aires office. It's in an hour."

"To discuss your new spokesmodel?"

Amadeo frowned. "You know about that?" He didn't remember telling his grandfather about his latest project.

"Yes, of course. Julio told me all about it. He showed me one of her photographs." Rodrigo nodded and there was a gleam of satisfaction in his eyes. "Good choice. You always had a good eye for beauty. The right kind of beauty. She has the look. Sophistication with a hint of defiance. The essence of the Aurora woman. I like that."

Amadeo cocked an eyebrow. The old man was perceptive, as always. He'd seen in Ellie exactly what had made Amadeo choose her. There was just something about her that drew you in. It was that something, that enigmatic quality, that would make consumers stop and take a second look. And that was what Cosmeticos Aurora needed, to get women hooked on the brand new make-up line that would take the company to the next level. Although already a multinational cosmetic giant, Amadeo had every intention of growing the business even more, and he wasn't afraid to go head-to-head with the worldwide market leaders. Revlon and L'Oreal, be warned.

But then Amadeo's thoughts turned back to what Rodrigo had said. He'd described Ellie's look as having a hint of defiance. Good for the Aurora look, no doubt, but that could also prove to be a problem. "Defiance is perfectly fine," he said, the deceptively cool tenor of his remark masking his true feelings, "as long as it's kept in check. I expect compliance from all members of my team."

Rodrigo chuckled. "I have the feeling you could have trouble with this one."

Amadeo cut him a sharp glance. He hadn't heard anything, had he? Still, as far as he was from the New York office, all the way in Buenos Aires, he would not put it past the office grapevine to go international.

But no, the old man's eyes were only filled with curiosity.

Amadeo decided to make his position unmistakably clear. "There'd better not be any trouble," he said, his voice brusque. "She already tested the waters. If it happens again she is out on her ear."

And no matter that she sparked his sexual curiosity – no, especially because of it – Amadeo meant every word.

53

CHAPTER SIX

"Wow." The word came out in a reverent whisper as Ellie turned around and around in the middle of the room. "This is a hotel suite?" She was talking to herself and if anyone could have seen her at that moment they would have thought she was crazy but she couldn't help it.

She'd arrived in Buenos Aires just two hours earlier, after an eleven-hour flight from New York City. She'd been transported from the airport in a stretch limousine, no less, and had been whisked off to the Alvear Palace Hotel. When Ellie saw it, there was one word that sprang to mind. Posh. The hotel was the picture of luxury and class.

The lobby, with its gleaming pink marble tiles and antique furniture, was impressive enough, but it was Ellie's private suite that took her breath away. It was huge, far larger than the three-bedroom apartment she shared with her family. The living room was spacious enough for her to host a party for over a dozen guests and the bedroom was no less grand. Here, she admired the canopied bed with its gold brocade coverlets and the matching drapes that adorned the windows.

A giggle escaped her lips. She climbed up and onto the king-sized bed then threw herself back into its firm softness. She spread her arms wide and did a snow angel right there in the middle of it. After the restriction of her twin-sized bed, the only practical size since two beds had to fit into the tiny room she shared with her sister, it was so freeing to be able to lay spread-eagle on the bed and still have tons of room to spare.

Still smiling, she rolled onto her stomach and reached over to where she'd dropped her cell phone on top of the night table. Time to call home. The phone rang two times then it clicked on, like someone had been nearby, awaiting the call.

"Hello?" It was Simone.

"Hey, Sport. What are you doing up?" It was nine-fifteen, just after her sister's bedtime.

"We've all been waiting for your call. Are you all right?"

On hearing the concern in Simone's voice, Ellie couldn't help smiling. Her little sister loved to play tough but she was such a soft-hearted little thing. "I'm fine, Simone. The flight was right on time and I'm at my hotel now. And guess what?"

"What?"

"This is the grandest hotel you ever saw. And my bedroom, it's so beautiful. You'd love it."

"Ooh! Can you send me pictures?" The worry had flown from Simone's voice and all Ellie could hear was unveiled excitement.

"Sure thing. You'll get some great ideas from this layout." Ellie would be only too happy to oblige. She knew Simone loved this sort of thing. Young though she was, she'd already begun to show interest in decorating and interior design. "Now go get Mom, Sport. It's after your bedtime and I don't want you staying up late because of me."

"Peter's right here. He wants to talk to you first. Can I put him on?"

"Of course. Let me talk to my little general." Then she chuckled. "Don't tell him I called him little."

But as soon as Peter came on the phone he dispelled her hope of keeping that comment secret. "I heard you," he said, using his deepest boy voice, "and I'm not little. I'm the biggest kid in my class."

"Okay. My bad. You're not little." Ellie bit her lip, intent on holding her laughter in. It would not do, when Peter was being so serious, to let him know how funny she was finding his protest. The fact was, no matter how big he got, he would always be her kid brother. "So how are you feeling, Pete?"

"I'm good. Mom took me to that neurofeedback training place today. I'm going to start my first session day after tomorrow."

"Good for you. It's going to help your brain to settle down so you won't have any more seizures. You'll see." Ellie spoke with confidence. She'd done enough research to feel reassured that this was the best treatment for Peter's condition. This brain training technique had calmed seizures in thousands of patients, making surgery unnecessary, which was a huge relief.

"They showed me the machines they'll hook me up to. It's computer screens with video games. They're gonna train me to control the video games with my brain. That's so cool."

This time Ellie could not hold back a happy laugh. Peter was actually excited about his treatment. "When I get back you can tell me all about it."

By this time Ellie could hear Abby's voice in the background. "Okay, guys. You've had your talk with Ellie. Time for bed."

"Aaw." That was Simone and it was obvious that she was nowhere near ready to turn in. "Can't we talk a little bit longer?"

"We'll talk to Ellie tomorrow. Now tell her goodbye and then let me have the phone."

"Bye, Ell. We'll call you tomorrow, okay?" Peter's voice was calm, almost nonchalant, a dead giveaway that he was doing his best not to sound emotional like a girl would, or like his sister was doing just then, pleading with their mother.

"Bye, Pete. I'll talk to you tomorrow. Love you."

His response to that was a grunt but Ellie didn't mind. She knew he loved her, too. He was just too much of an adolescent boy to say it.

Simone came back on the phone. "Bye, bye, Ellie. I miss you."

"I miss you, too, sweetie. We'll talk tomorrow and that will help. All right?"

"All right," she replied, her tone one of grudging acceptance. "And remember to send me the pictures."

"I will."

When Abby came on the phone she gave a soft sigh. "Those two, they insisted they weren't going to bed until they spoke to you. God help me if your flight had been delayed."

"Mmm." Ellie murmured her agreement. "Sounds like you've been having one of those days with them."

"You've got that right. Since you left for the airport this morning they've been on edge, asking me every ten minutes when you're going to call. Even Kevin's been asking for you, running into your room and calling your name."

Just the picture of it, her little brother searching the apartment for her, made her heart melt. She loved them so much. "I can hardly wait till I get back home to you guys. I just got here but I miss you already."

"And we miss you, too," Abby quickly responded, "but you're in Argentina for a purpose and you're doing a world of good for your family. You should be proud."

Ellie sighed. "I am, but-"

"No 'buts'. It's because of you that I was able to register Peter for the neurofeedback therapy. Did he tell you?"

"Yes, he told me he was there today."

"Thanks to you, I made the deposit and he'll start training in two days. You handed the money over, just like that. You're so selfless and I'm...so proud of you." Abby's voice cracked as she said the words.

For a moment Ellie was quiet and then she said softly, "No thanks to me, Mom. It's all thanks to Amadeo."

"Yes, he was very generous to give you that advance. But remember, it was not a gift. You'll be earning it back while you're working for him."

"I know, but still..." Even as she thought about it, Ellie raised her eyebrows. "To give me five thousand dollars just like that, out of the blue? I never expected it."

"No, but that's how blessings come, at the most unexpected times and in the most unexpected ways."

"And just when you need them."

"Just when you need them," her mother repeated. "And, for that, I give thanks."

At Abby's words, Ellie could feel the emotions welling up inside her. She cleared her throat. "I'm just glad Peter won't have to do that awful surgery. Can you believe the doctor, suggesting he could sever the band of nerves between the two brain hemispheres? Just the thought of it gives me the shivers."

"I know." Abby sounded just as horrified. "That's the treatment they've used for severe epilepsy but thank God we now have an alternative. And they say it helps kids with ADD, too."

"Attention Deficit Disorder? But I thought they prescribed drugs for that."

"They do, but the center told me neurofeedback training is also effective with some kids with ADD, the primarily inattentive kind. For parents who aren't comfortable with putting their kids on medication, this is a great alternative."

"Good to know."

"You never know," Abby continued, "this therapy may help Peter in more ways than one."

"That's a good point," Ellie began then she broke off as her phone began to beep. "Hold on, Mom. There's another call coming in." She tapped the screen to accept the other call. "Hello?"

"Hello, Ellie. Welcome to Argentina."

At the sound of Amadeo's deep, heavily accented voice, Ellie's heart jerked. She hadn't expected him to call her tonight, not at this late hour. It must be the surprise of hearing his voice that had her heart beating like a drum. "Amadeo...I...thank you." She sounded flustered but he'd caught her off guard. Who could blame her? "I...I have my mother on the other line. Could you hold a moment, please?" Not waiting for his answer, she switched over to the other line. "Mom, it's Amadeo. I have to go but I'll call you in the morning, okay?"

"Okay, sweetheart. Rest well."

"Thanks, Mom. You, too." She clicked back to Amadeo. "Sorry about that," she said, trying her best to sound more relaxed. "I'm with you now."

"That's fine," he said, his voice rumbling into the phone. "I called to let you know that you will not be expected to work tomorrow. You may rest and then in the afternoon you'll be taken for a tour of the city. I want you to get to know Buenos Aires. As the representative of Cosmeticos Aurora you must get a feel for our city, our culture."

For some strange reason, at his words Ellie's heart did another flip. She'd be touring the city tomorrow. Would it be with him? And then, on realizing her folly, she drew in her breath. What was she getting excited about? Spending time with a man who could hardly be described as pleasant? Really, Ellie?

And then she also realized how stupid she was being. Why would a powerful man like Amadeo Castillo waste his time chauffeuring her around the city?

His next words confirmed what she was thinking. "Ernesto will pick you up after lunch," he said, "at one-thirty. Make sure you're ready. He has instructions to have you back at the hotel on the dot of six."

Ellie frowned. "Why?"

"That will give you enough time to get ready. I will be picking you up at seven o'clock for dinner."

Just like that. She was to go out to dinner with Amadeo. He hadn't invited her. He was pretty much ordering her.

And the way he'd done it almost made Ellie laughed. What was this man's problem? Did he think he should always be bossing people around?

Feeling daring, she decided to ask a facetious question. "Do I have a choice?" It was a pointed question but, to take the edge off, she spoke with a smile in her voice.

She thought her playful tone would have made him laugh, made him realize how inappropriate his stern tone had been. Maybe he would apologize for giving an order instead of making a request.

She was wrong.

His response was quick and sharp. "No, you don't," he said, with not a hint of apology in his voice. "You are to be ready by seven. Do not be late. Have a good night." And with that terse command he hung up the phone, not even giving Ellie a chance to respond.

"Well." It was all she could say as she drew the cell phone from her ear and clicked it off.

In giving her the unexpected pay advance Amadeo had been generous and she'd begun to think well of him. Now she realized the man was as much of a jerk as he'd always been.

And it didn't look like he'd be changing any time soon.

· · ❧ · ·

EVEN AS HE TAPPED THE screen to end the call, Amadeo knew the conversation hadn't gone exactly as he'd intended. He'd meant to be firm but he'd come across like *un pendejo* instead. A real jerk.

Scowling, he threw the phone onto the bed and stalked across the room, shrugging off the terry cloth bathrobe and letting it fall to the floor. He needed some air.

Dressed in nothing but his silk boxer shorts, he opened the glass sliding door and stepped out onto his private balcony. It was only when he'd crossed the tiles and was leaning over the railing, drawing in the fragrance of the night air, that he began to relax. What was it about Ellie Goldwell that had him wound tight as a spring?

As he stared down at the city of Buenos Aires from the balcony of his penthouse apartment he tightened his lips. It must have been that conversation with his *abuelo* that put him in a worse mood than usual. The old man had predicted trouble. He'd seen something in Ellie's eyes, something that told him this girl would not be easy to control.

Amadeo had seen it, too, that light in her eyes, the reflection of a spirit that would be hard to break.

Not that he wanted to break her. No, it was that spirit that intrigued him, made him want to know more. It was a feeling that worried him.

His relationship with Ellie was strictly on a professional level. So why the hell did his heart tighten at the thought of seeing her again?

CHAPTER SEVEN

A s ordered, Ellie was ready when Ernesto pulled up in front of the hotel at one-thirty in the afternoon. Thank goodness he hadn't come in the stretch limo this time. Instead, he was driving a black Cadillac Escalade SUV but he was just as smartly dressed as he'd been the evening before, in black suit and stark-white shirt, and sporting the same warm smile with which he'd greeted her at the airport. *"Buenos dias, senorita.* I hope you rested well." His smile widened as he opened the passenger door and gave her his arm so that she could climb in.

"Very well, thank you," she replied and returned the smile. She liked Ernesto. At least six or seven inches taller than she was and with at least a hundred pound advantage, he was a big man, but so genteel that she felt totally comfortable with him. She settled into the vehicle and when he came around to the driver's side and climbed in she cocked her head to one side. "Where to?" she asked.

He turned the key in the ignition then glanced at her. "First, the Palermo, one of the most popular areas in all of Buenos Aires. We will visit the plazas, the botanical gardens and the park. I'm sure you'll enjoy them."

Ernesto was right. When they got to Palermo, Ellie was soon lost in the enchanting beauty of the gardens. Her guide had a hard time pulling her away from its one hundred and seventy year old national monument.

"We must go, *senorita*," he urged. "There are still many places to see and the time will fly quickly. I must get you back by six. Not much time."

He seemed so concerned that Ellie gave in and climbed back into the car without protest. The last thing she wanted to do was to make him get in trouble with his boss.

Their next stop was Plaza de Mayo where Ellie saw the grand and beautiful Casa Rosada, the most photographed building in all of Buenos Aires. She was surprised to learn that, although it was called the presidential house, the president did not live there but only came there for work. It was from a north balcony of this building that the renowned president, Eva Peron, played by Madonna in the 1996 movie *Evita,* spoke to adoring crowds.

To Ellie's disappointment, Ernesto did not allow her to complete the tour of the museum housed inside Casa Rosada. "We must go, I'm afraid." His tone was apologetic. "We do not have much time."

He was right. They'd only made two stops but already it was after four o'clock. Where had the afternoon gone? "Where are we going now?" she asked.

"We only have time for one more stop. Recoleta."

It turned out that Recoleta was well worth the visit. The home of the city's aristocracy, it featured pricey apartments occupied by the super-wealthy of Argentina. Ellie did the walking tour of the neighborhood, from the Recoleta Cemetery with its impressive family mausoleums to Nuestra Senora del Pilar Basilica, a church built in 1732 which housed altarpieces and artwork which had been impeccably preserved over the centuries.

It was only when Ernesto drove the SUV up Avenida Ayacucho then turned left and pulled up in front of Alvear Palace Hotel that she realized that, the whole time they'd been touring Recoleta, they'd actually been right there in the hotel's neighborhood.

"We have made it," Ernesto announced with a wide grin, "right on time."

She glanced at the clock on the dashboard. It was exactly six o'clock. Shaking her head, she grinned back at him. "You scare me. Too perfect."

He only laughed then hopped out and came around to help her out of the car.

"Thank you for a wonderful afternoon," Ellie told him as she took his hand and slid off her seat.

"It was my pleasure," he said with a bow, looking like he meant every word.

Why couldn't Amadeo be like this, even a little bit? The thought slipped into her consciousness before she could put up her defenses. In an effort to hide her confusion, she gave Ernesto an extra-bright smile and a wave then hurried up the steps and into the lobby of the hotel before he could see her face and wonder why she looked so pink and flustered.

She was grateful that she was alone as she rode the elevator up to her floor. As soon as she entered her suite she pushed the door shut behind her, leaned back against it and let out a soft sigh. Yes, the afternoon had been great. The one thing that spoiled it was when Amadeo invaded her mind. Why did this man dominate her thoughts? Why should she even care what he was like? As long as he stayed out of her way and let her do her job it didn't matter how much of a grouch he was.

Annoyed at herself for even sparing him a thought, she pushed away from the door and strode across the living room. A nice soak in the Jacuzzi tub was exactly what she needed to ease the tension. She was stripping off her clothes even before she got to the bathroom, leaving a trail of shirt, bra, and shorts strung out on the floor behind her. Minutes later, she was sinking into a whirlpool of warm water, its surface covered with a fragrant frost of bubbles.

A soft sigh escaped her lips as she rested the back of her head against the lip of the tub. Heaven.

As she'd known it would, the soothing soak had her relaxed and mellow in no time. She slid even lower in the water, reveling in its warmth, letting her mind slip into that sweet state of blissful emptiness.

Too soon, she had to do a time check. Reluctantly, she cracked one eye open, expecting that only nine or ten minutes had passed. The clock showed six twenty-one. Ellie gasped and jerked upright. Holy geez. She had to move fast if she wasn't going to be late. The last thing she wanted was to give that man reason to chew her out.

She jumped up and out of the tub, splashing water everywhere, but she had no time to worry about that. Ripping a towel off the rack as she rushed by, she rubbed the water from her skin as she headed for the closet. Red dress, gold dress, black dress, sequins. She grabbed the simplest one she could find, a black shift with spaghetti straps, one that would say she was all business.

Within twenty minutes of hopping out of the tub, Ellie was ready. Even though she was in the beauty business she didn't spend a lot of time on make-up. When she wasn't in front of the camera she went for simplicity. Especially tonight. She wanted to show Amadeo that she felt no obligation to dress to impress – not her body and not her face. He would see that, as far as she was concerned, he was no-one special. Boss or no boss, he was just a man like any other.

Yeah, Ellie. Keep telling yourself that...Oh, shut up, will you? She shook her head, trying to clear the warring thoughts from her mind. Okay, so she was sort of attracted to him. Just a teeny tiny bit. That much she would admit to herself. Despite his boorish attitude there was something about Amadeo that made her pulse race. And it annoyed the heck out of her.

And that was why, when the glass doors at the entrance to the hotel lobby opened and Amadeo walked in, he found her standing there with a fierce frown on her face.

"Good evening." He walked up to her as she stood by the elegant flower-filled vase decorating the lobby entrance. His gray eyes, as cool as the mist over a frosty pond, roamed over her then settled on her face. His eyes narrowed...or was she imagining it? Tilting his head, he gave her a slight bow. "Shall we go?"

She gave him a nod as curt as the one he'd given her. "Of course." He hadn't commented on the way she looked. Not that she'd expected him to. It wasn't like they were going out on a date. This was a business meeting.

Side by side, they walked back toward the exit then Amadeo stepped aside so that she could precede him. At least in that, he was acting the gentleman. When they got to his car, a sleek, silver Jaguar, he held the door open and, as she moved to enter, he took her hand.

It was the third time he'd touched her and this time, instead of cupping her chin, his hand enveloped hers. It was a big hand, a strong one, and it made her feel no less vulnerable than when he'd touched her that first time.

She wouldn't let him know that, though. Doing everything in her power to seem composed, she gave him a polite smile as she slid onto the creamy white leather seat. It was only when he released her, stepped back and closed the door that she began to breathe again.

By the time Amadeo walked around the car and slid onto the seat beside her, Ellie's pulse had slowed and she was almost back to normal. When he started the engine then turned to look at her she was back to the state she'd been practicing all evening, Miss Cool and Collected.

"We have reservations at La Bourgogne", he said. "The food there is *magnifico*. You will enjoy it."

Why wasn't she surprised he'd said that? Not, 'I hope you'll enjoy it'. No, that would have been too obliging for Amadeo Castillo. He had to be decisive about everything.

Even as they drove away from the hotel, she didn't reply. He'd already made up his mind what her reaction should be so, whether she agreed with him or not, it didn't matter. Besides, she had other, more important issues on her mind...like how to keep up this 'cool and collected' act when she was having a hard time breathing. She was breathing, of course, but her chest was just a tad too tight and her breaths just a little bit jagged. And it was all Amadeo's fault...even if he didn't know it.

The problem was, she wasn't used to being in such close quarters with a man who made her blood boil...unfortunately, in more ways than one. And why he was having this effect on her, she had absolutely no idea. He wasn't even a likable man, with his arrogant attitude and imperious manner. The one time she'd thought of revising her opinion of him, he'd dashed that idea as soon as he started talking. A leopard could never change his spots.

Annoyed with herself, Ellie gave a soft hiss and shifted in her seat.

At the sound, Amadeo shifted his gaze from the road for a millisecond. "Is there a problem?"

"No, everything's fine." She gave him a tight smile, hoping that would reassure him, then turned her head ever so slightly so she could gaze out the window and away from him. Feigning intense interest in the Buenos Aires streets, she gazed at the scenery flitting by, hoping he wouldn't try to draw her into conversation. She was not feeling up to it.

She needn't have worried. For the next few minutes Amadeo was as silent as she was, his attention focused on navigating the busy Buenos Aires streets on a Tuesday evening. Or that was what he wanted her to believe. Before looking away she'd seen the tight set of his jaw and his slight frown, which told her otherwise. There was something bothering him. Maybe she was his problem. Not chatty enough, perhaps? Well, she was in no mood for small talk, especially not with him, so he would just have to deal with it.

Thankfully, the trip to La Bourgogne took just a little over ten minutes and soon they'd entered the restaurant and were being ushered toward a private, elegantly decorated alcove. It was only after he'd held her chair so that she could take her seat, then positioned himself across from her, that she saw an almost imperceptible change in him. There was the slightest softening of his features, as if he'd just begun to relax. If this had been another man she would have guessed that, in the car, he'd been as tightly wound as she'd been. But Amadeo? Never. He wasn't quite so human.

As soon as the *camarero* took their orders and departed, Amadeo got down to business. "I invited you to dinner so that we could discuss the project and the plans I have for its execution."

Ellie raised an eyebrow but, tempted though she was, she refrained from commenting on his choice of the word 'invited'. They both knew how untrue that was. "Your plans?" she asked, then waited for him to elaborate.

"You've already done the New York photo shoot so you know what is expected of you. However, here in Argentina we will do things differently."

That got Ellie's attention. She cocked her head to one side. "What do you mean?"

Amadeo sat back in his chair, a satisfied smile on his lips. He was obviously enjoying the fact that he'd piqued her curiosity. "For the Argentina photo shoot I want a more earthy look and feel. You must be one with the country, the culture and the brand. I want you to live, breathe and feel the brand. You are Aurora."

She frowned. "What does that mean?"

"Do you know who Aurora is?"

She shook her head. "I have no idea."

"A Roman goddess. The goddess of the dawn. That is who you will be. You will be our Aurora." He spoke the words in a low voice, sounding so solemn that Ellie almost took him seriously.

But not quite. "Me? Aurora? I don't know about that." She began to chuckle but the look he gave her made the laughter die on her lips. Clearly, he was not amused.

When he spoke again his tone was harsh, with not a hint of the animation he'd displayed earlier. Now he was just the boss, giving orders. "As you get to know Argentina you will also learn as much as you can about Aurora. If you are to be my spokesmodel you must personify my brand. I expect nothing less."

It was a tall order, to be sure, but Ellie didn't bother to tell him that. As far as she was concerned she'd been hired to be a model, not an actress, but she wouldn't remind Amadeo. Not just now. Why stir up the hornet's nest before she had to?

And so she listened quietly while the man who paid her wages spoke about plans to travel to different locales across Argentina where they would get shots of her against a variety of backgrounds. It sounded like she would have her work cut out for her, fitting into a variety of scenes, but she didn't question him, not even once. Now was not the time.

He was in the middle of telling her about a photo shoot scheduled to take place at Palacio Barolo, a stately ministerial edifice with the ideal air of ageless sophistication, when the meal arrived. He waited patiently while the *camarero* slipped the plates onto the table in front of them.

Amadeo looked up at the young man. "*Muchas gracias. Se ve bien.*"

The server, looking surprised, nodded quickly then his face broke into a smile. Backing away, he nodded again then turned and headed back the way he'd come.

Ellie raised her eyebrows. "*Se ve bien?*"

"It looks good." He glanced across at her plate and then down at his own. "I wasn't lying."

She glanced down, too. "No, you weren't," she murmured but the savory barbecued beef with steamed vegetables were not what was on her mind. Her curiosity would not let it rest. "Why did the server seem so surprised when you told him that?"

It was her turn to be surprised when Amadeo gave her a look that seemed to have a tinge of regret. If it had been any other man she would have described his look as sheepish. Somehow, though, Amadeo and sheepish did not fit comfortably in the same sentence.

He gave her a rueful grin. "Last time I was here I wasn't the most pleasant of patrons. I have a reputation for being a *cascarrabias*." He wrinkled his nose. "In English, I think you would call that a grouch."

Ellie laughed, not even trying to hide her amusement. "Now why am I not surprised?"

Amadeo's lips curled into a crooked smile, his normally furrowed brow relaxing and his granite eyes softening. "Are you saying you agree with them?"

Without hesitation, she nodded. "Absolutely. I couldn't agree with them more."

"Ah ha." He said this slowly, softly, his eyes seeming to go all serious again. "Then I must prove you wrong."

And the way he said the words, the way he was looking at her, eyes hooded, made Ellie wonder what in the world he meant.

. . ❧ . .

AMADEO COULD HAVE KICKED himself for letting that slip. He would have to prove her wrong? How the *diablo* was he going to do that? He was who he was, and he had no plans to change for anybody.

And yet, this woman sitting across from him, the subdued light casting a soft glow over her skin and making her look lovelier than ever, was making him have second thoughts. Cold and brutal though he might be, for some strange reason he wanted Ellie to see that, beyond the hardened surface, there was more. He wasn't just the tyrant she'd come to know. Underneath it all he was a man...

...a man who, with each passing moment, was falling more and more under her spell.

Amadeo frowned. Another wayward thought. What the devil was wrong with him tonight? He had no business letting his mind wander down that path. Ellie Goldwell was off limits, someone who now worked for him. He knew he would do well to remember that.

He was so annoyed at himself that he could feel the scowl creeping back onto his face. Before he scared her off he picked up his fork then forced a smile onto his lips. "*Bon appetit.*"

She must have seen the scowl because she hesitated then, almost imperceptibly, her lips tightened. She picked up her fork. "*Bon appetit,*" she replied, but there was no smile in her voice. The moment they'd shared, the easy laughter, that was gone.

Amadeo turned his attention to the beef steak on his plate, even as he did an inward shrug. So much for playing 'nice guy'. He'd given it a try and had failed so quickly.

As the Americans would say, when it came to being pleasant, he sucked.

CHAPTER EIGHT

What was the matter with him? Amadeo was turning out to be the hardest man Ellie had ever had to figure out.

Her first impression had been that he was a pompous, overbearing jerk. That hadn't changed until he'd surprised her with the unexpected advance that made it possible for her to start the payments for Peter's therapy. Then he'd gone back to being arrogant. And then, just when she'd accepted the fact that her first impression was the right one, he'd turned mysterious, almost...seductive, confusing her when he'd given her that look then said he would prove her wrong.

And now this. Within seconds of a fairly pleasant exchange he'd gone right back to his old self, frowning at her like she'd done something wrong. She could just imagine how the rest of this dinner meeting would go. She was dying for it to end.

"How is it?"

"Excuse me?" Ellie glanced up from the plate where she'd been busy cutting off her second piece of beef.

"The steak. How is it?"

"Mmm. Very good. Delicious, actually."

"Good. I'm glad you like it." Amadeo looked like he meant it. "It's been prepared in typical Argentine fashion, basted with *chimichurri* grilling sauce.

"*Chimichurri*. Did I say that right?"

"Perfect. Are you sure you don't have a touch of the Argentine in you?" To Ellie's surprise, Amadeo actually smiled when he said that. It looked like his mood was lifting, after all.

Not one hundred percent sure of him, she gave him a tentative smile. "Not that I know of." Then, wanting to take the focus off her, she asked, "So what makes *chimichurri* taste so good?"

"It is a mixture of onion, garlic, oregano, salt and pepper in an olive oil and vinegar base. For grilled meat, it's a must."

"So you're having it, too?"

He chuckled. "I am having it, too, but I'm sure you could not handle my version. Mine was basted two additional times with lots of cayenne pepper. Super spicy, just the way I like it." Then he popped a piece of meat into his mouth and as he chewed, his gaze never left her face.

Ellie dropped her eyes. Were they still talking about the meat on his plate?

She reached for her glass and took a slow slip of red wine, eager to steady her nerves. At this point she didn't know which she preferred, when he was being crude or when he was being smooth. Either way, he was a disconcerting man.

A sudden thought came to her. She could be disarming, too. She would just throw the spotlight back on him. "Tell me more about Argentina," she said, "and about you. After all, what better way to learn about the culture and the people than to interview the Argentine I'm most familiar with?"

Amadeo cocked an eyebrow but then he swallowed and reached for his glass of wine. He took his own sweet time, savoring the mellow liquid before he spoke. "What do you want to know?"

As she thought about it, Ellie lifted her napkin to dab at her lips. "Let's see," she drawled, buying time as she decided what to ask. There was a lot she wanted to know about the country and now that she'd been given this opportunity, there was a lot she wanted to know about Amadeo. But how personal could she get? Then she had an idea. She would ask about a time when all was innocence. She was sure he wouldn't mind sharing that. "What was it like," she asked, "growing up in Argentina? I'd love to hear about a typical Argentine childhood."

He'd been about to take another sip of wine but he paused then slowly returned his glass to the table. Tilting his head to one side, he looked at her, his gray eyes darkening with an emotion that was unreadable. "A typical Argentine childhood? I am sorry. I cannot help you there."

Ellie laid her napkin on the table then sat forward, just a little bit. Amadeo was the one who'd asked what she wanted to know. Now he was playing secretive? She wasn't about to let that happen. "Okay, maybe your childhood wasn't typical, what with you being from a super-rich family. But surely you can tell me about what it was like for a child growing up in Argentina."

For some strange reason it seemed like that was the hardest question she could have asked him. Amadeo's glance fell to the wine glass in front of him and he reached out to press his thumb and index finger around its stem. Slowly, he began to twirl it. "I did not have a typical childhood," he said, "because I did not have a typical family. I became a man when I was eleven years old."

Ellie frowned. "You...what happened?"

"I lost my mother to cancer. After that, I was alone. I had to grow up fast."

"But where was your father?" Her eyes widened. "Did something happen to him, too?"

Amadeo's lips curled then he made a sound that was a cross between a grunt and a chuckle. "Yes, something happened to him. He abandoned me for his dream of becoming the world's greatest gambler." He lifted his gaze and when she looked into his eyes what she saw there was bitterness and pain. "When I lost my mother I lost everything. My father was dead to me, too. So, typical childhood? I did not have this. Not unless you consider near starvation typical."

"Near...starvation? What do you mean?" Ellie's heart tightened inside. What can of worms had she just opened? What in the world had Amadeo gone through?

He shook his head. "No. Forgive me. I will say no more." His jaw turned rigid, he sat back in his chair and looked away, like he was searching for the *camarero*.

But Ellie wasn't having it. "No, you will say more. How can you say something like that then shut up? What do you mean, near starvation? Did your father abuse you?"

Amadeo raised his eyebrows then his lips curled again but this time she could see that the smile actually reached his eyes. "Now who is being bossy? I thought that was my job."

Involuntarily, her lips curled into an answering smile. "Until I get some answers, I'm the boss."

Still smiling, he shrugged. "Very well. I will give you your answer." He nodded, as if to confirm his decision. "You asked if I'd been abused. Not in the typical sense of the word. He never raised a hand to me, never locked me inside the house. I could have walked out the door at any time. Now, if you ask me if he neglected me, then I must say yes. After Mama died it was as if he did not remember I existed."

Mama. The way he said the word, with just a hint of a pause after it, told Ellie a whole lot more than he was saying aloud. She didn't need a degree in psychology to know that, although so many years had passed, Amadeo still loved his mother very much. It was another chink in his armor, a crack that exposed a tiny sliver of his humanity.

Her heart going out to the grief-stricken child he must have been, Ellie shook her head. "How did you manage?"

"I managed," he said, his tone matter-of-fact. "I was a fast learner. I came to understand that, whenever he was around, I should ask for as much as I could get. In that way I could afford to get food when he was away. That is how I survived for several months."

Ellie gasped. "My God. Months?"

"Yes, until I was placed into the care of my grandfather."

"So where was this grandfather of yours all that time? Didn't he know what was going on?"

Amadeo gave her a look of amusement. "There is no need to be angry with my *abuelo* or with anybody. No-one knew what was going on. I was the one who chose to keep that secret."

"You were a child," she hissed. "You didn't know what you were doing."

"I knew exactly what I was doing. I was being independent. I was learning to be a man."

Ellie drew in a slow breath and as she did so she was shaking her head. "You should never have had to learn independence in that way."

"I do not regret it, trying to grow up on my own. It has made me the man I am today." And with those words, Amadeo sat forward and picked up his fork. "I have answered your question. Now we must eat before our food grows cold."

After that their conversation was tame but, curious though she was, she did not question Amadeo further. He'd deliberately brought the discussion to an end and she guessed he had his reasons. She would just have to let it rest, at least for the time being.

And so, instead of talking about Amadeo they spoke about Argentina, the people, the music, the food, the culture. It was important, Amadeo said, that she should be comfortable with her new environment. For them to be able to do successful photo shoots she had to play the part and play it well. So Ellie listened, and then she asked questions, about everything and anything but Amadeo.

By the time he called for the bill, Ellie felt like a virtual authority on all things Argentina. And she was exhausted. It had been a long day.

When Amadeo stood and gave her his arm she did not object. He must have picked up on her tired state because their walk out of the restaurant and back to the car was leisurely. She was grateful. As tired as she was, and in the four inch high heels she was wearing, leisurely was all she could manage.

As they crossed the parking lot, the coolness of the night chilled Ellie's bare arms and she shivered.

Amadeo glanced down at her. "Cold?"

She shook her head. "No, I'm fine." It was a lie but the last thing she wanted to do was to seem vulnerable. And anyway, if she said yes what would he do about it? Play gallant gentleman and whip off his jacket so he could drape it around her shoulders? She didn't see that happening. That was definitely not Amadeo.

But then, just as they got to the car, she shivered again and without thinking she leaned into him, drawing in his warmth.

And then Amadeo did the unexpected. As if her sudden closeness triggered a response in him he slid his palms up her arms and those hands, so large and warm, made her shiver again, this time in a good way. The feel of his hands, so delicious against her skin, made a soft sigh escape her lips.

Ellie tilted her face up to gaze into Amadeo's eyes and what she saw there made her heart pick up pace. Was he feeling it, too? This magnetic pull that had her yearning to have his arms around her? The look in his eyes, now smoky-gray, told her, without a doubt, that their closeness was affecting him, too.

As if of their own volition her eyelids fluttered closed, her lips parting softly, and when she felt Amadeo's arms encircle her she knew he would give her what she craved. All this time she'd been suppressing her feelings, hiding them from herself, but there was just something about this man that she could not resist. She shouldn't give in to the attraction. She mustn't. All of that, she knew. But right now she would live in the moment. She wanted this too much to say no.

And then Amadeo's lips touched hers and all thoughts flew from her mind. Softly, gently, he stroked her lips with his. Was this the Amadeo who had always been so forceful? With his kiss he was showing her a new side of him, a seductively sensual side that had her melting in his arms.

As a soft moan escaped her lips he drew her closer, his lips covering hers. Then he took control, his gentleness giving way to a more urgent pressure until she yielded to him, her lips parting for him, her hands sliding up to grasp his rock-solid arms.

Even as Amadeo kissed her, the thoughts were a swirling whirlpool in her head. *We shouldn't do this. This is wrong. Too wrong. But I want this…so much. Please don't stop.*

But, as was the way with all good things, the kiss did come to an end. Amadeo lifted his head and relaxed his arms, letting them fall away from her, then he stepped back.

It was only then that Ellie opened her eyes. Her gaze flew to his face. What would she see there?

Amadeo was looking down at her, his gray eyes unreadable, his lips curled in a rueful and slightly sardonic smile. "Forgive me," he said. "That should never have happened. Please accept my apologies."

He was so formal, with even the hint of a smile disappearing from his face, that Ellie's heart slowly sank to the pit of her stomach. Amadeo had not been moved by the kiss. Was she the only one who'd felt it? That jolt, as if from a lightning bolt, when their lips touched?

He was moving away now, stepping back to open the passenger door for her, and all Ellie could do was nod and slide onto the seat. When he closed the door, the sound of the click was not just a door closing. It was a signal that the evening had come to an end.

And the kiss that had brought that evening to a close? It had been a huge mistake.

At the thought, her spirit sank even lower. The kiss? She now knew that it meant nothing to Amadeo. So why did it mean so much to her?

.. ❦ ..

IT WAS A SUBDUED ELLIE who got up next morning and readied herself to face the day. She'd tossed and turned all night as she played and replayed the evening with Amadeo in her mind. Thank heavens she wasn't scheduled for a photo shoot. With the bags that had formed under her eyes, the photographer would certainly have cause for complaint.

The driver who came to get her was a plump, gray-haired man with round cheeks and smiling eyes. "*Mucho gusto en conocerle, senorita*. I am Raul and I'm pleased to meet you."

"Good morning, Raul. I'm pleased to meet you, too." She shook his hand. "Where is Ernesto?"

"It is his day off. I am happy about that." He smiled as he held the door open so she could get into the SUV.

"Oh? Why is that?" As she lifted her legs into the car she looked up at him.

"Because he has given me the opportunity to spend the next twenty minutes with the most beautiful woman in the world." His smile widened, making the soft crow's feet at the corner of his eyes crinkle. He was still chuckling as he circled the car then climbed in. "Forgive me, *senorita*. This is how I am. I cannot tell a lie."

Ellie laughed. Raul had a gift for making her feel good and if there was any time she needed that, it was this morning. She could do with a boost before she faced Amadeo again.

At the offices of Cosmeticos Aurora she was escorted into an elegant lobby then met by a slender, dark-haired woman who looked like a model, herself. "I am Vera," she said, "Amadeo's creative director for the Latin America division. I will show you around the office and then we will get started."

"Get started? Are we doing a photo shoot today?" She wasn't ready for a shoot. Not today. Ellie could only hope she had heard wrong.

"No, of course not." Vera stepped aside and ushered her into the elevator. "I am talking about your meeting with the advertising department. Today you will meet all the key players. These are the people who will be turning you into a star." As she said the last word she raised a graceful arm into the air and twirled her fingers. "They are all looking forward to meeting the special person that Amadeo has chosen to be our spokesmodel."

"Oh. I see. I didn't know that." Ellie leaned back against the elevator wall and drew in a surreptitious breath, steeling herself for what was to come. She'd never been good with crowds. She could only hope the meeting would include only two or three people. And why hadn't Amadeo mentioned this meeting? All he'd said at dinner was that she would be visiting his office the next day. A visit was one thing but a meeting with his advertising team was a whole different kettle of fish.

For the next twenty minutes Ellie followed Vera around the office, touring the facilities. It was an impressive building, eleven stories tall with a majestic fountain set right in the middle of it. Unlike the typical office building, this one was full of light, the results of the abundance of glass that made up its structure.

"The aesthetics of the building reflects our business philosophy," Vera told her. "Glamour, sophistication and charm, all in one package. That is what we offer today's woman. That is how we empower her."

Ellie raised her eyebrows but she said nothing. It did sound like something Amadeo would say. He was all about empowerment. For himself, anyway.

After the tour, Vera took her to a large conference room on the seventh floor. "Make yourself comfortable," she said. "We're twelve minutes early. The advertising group will be coming in soon." She waved her hand in the direction of a sideboard laden with muffins, doughnuts and fresh fruit. "Help yourself. I will be back in a minute."

Ellie did not help herself nor did she make herself comfortable. Instead, she slowly crossed the room until she was standing by the ceiling-to-floor window that looked out onto the courtyard. She was still standing there when the first of the meeting participants arrived. It was a small, red-haired woman whose huge glasses gave her the look of a wise little owl. "I'm Margaret," she said, "a transplant from Arkansas. I'm one of the copy writers." She stuck her hand out.

Ellie took it for a quick handshake. "I'm happy to meet you, Margaret." Then, curious, she asked, "So how many copy writers are on your team?"

"Eleven." Spying the table of goodies, Margaret turned and headed for it.

"Eleven? And they're all coming to the meeting?"

"No, just the lead writers." Margaret grabbed a doughnut and took a bite. Ellie was in the middle of a sigh of relief when she continued. "That would be four of us. And then there are the graphic artists, the brand managers and the account executives."

Ellie's gaze narrowed. " So how many of them are there?"

Margaret's lips moved as she did a quick calculation. "That will make fourteen in all."

Ellie gritted her teeth. That was a crowd. She could already feel her palms growing damp.

But Margaret was not done yet. "And then, of course, there are the managers."

Ellie swallowed. "Managers? How many?"

"Oh, not many. Vera will be in the meeting, of course. And Pedro, our head of marketing, and Isabel who leads the sales team. That's it." She gave Ellie a bright smile. "So, how long have you been in Argentina? Did you get a chance to go sightseeing?"

Before she could respond, three people walked in. Margaret introduced them as Jim, Emilio and Cesar from the graphics department. By the time those introductions were over another set of employees arrived, and then another, and soon Ellie found herself shaking so many hands, she lost count. She only knew that, with each person she met, she became a little bit more tense.

As she contemplated that annoying weakness of hers, she fought the urge to shake her head. It was so strange, the way she could hold her own in a one-to-one battle, but then seized up when she had to face a throng.

Once the meeting started, though, she realized that she needn't have worried. Although the conference room was crowded, the advertising team didn't let it bother them. A couple of them went and got their own chairs and pushed them into the room. They came across as an easygoing group of people and the atmosphere in the room was so relaxed that Ellie felt her tension begin to ease. There were still the same number of people surrounding her but now they didn't seem quite so intimidating.

"We'd like to share with you our vision for the brand," the director of marketing explained. "If you understand this, then you will take our message to the world." As Pedro spoke in his heavily accented English he waved his hand toward the cosmetics on display at the front of the room. Ellie had to concentrate to understand all that he was saying but she was grateful that he was making the effort to speak in English so she could understand. They all were. She hadn't expected Amadeo's staff to be so accommodating. It was the strangest thing but these employees were nothing like their leader.

By the time the meeting had been in progress for an hour Ellie was so comfortable with the group that she was laughing at the stories they were sharing. Apparently, being on the road week after week, going from photo shoot to photo shoot, was not as easy as she'd thought. And the models they'd had on their projects, some of them real divas, hadn't made the job any easier. When she heard the groans of the team members she resolved to be the easiest model they'd ever worked with. For being so nice to her in the meeting, she owed them that much.

"You will be our Kate Hudson," Vera said, an excited glow in her eyes. "She is spokesmodel for Almay. She represents the brand perfectly. You will do the same for us."

Isabel nodded. "It is a mother-daughter duo. Goldie Hawn also represents the brand." Her lips curled into a crooked smile. "Are you hiding a mother as beautiful as you? We have a skin firming crème that could do with some support."

They all laughed at that. Isabel was joking, of course. Still, it was sweet of her to even mention her mother as a potential candidate.

The laughter was just dying down when there was a sharp rap at the conference room door. They all looked up as it opened and Amadeo strolled in. "How is it going?" he asked as he headed toward the front of the room. "I hope the discussions have been productive."

"Yes, of course," Vera said with a nod, surprising Ellie because she seemed so comfortable with Amadeo. Wasn't she the least bit intimidated by his brusque manner? "We have brought Ellie up-to-date on our expectations," she continued, "and she has assured us that she can and will deliver. We have every confidence that she will."

It was only at the mention of her name that Amadeo turned his gaze in Ellie's direction. As his gray eyes zoned in on her she felt her heart give a tiny flutter. After the kiss they'd shared the night before, what thoughts were going through his mind? Had he relived their kiss, over and over again, as she had? And now, as he gazed at her, was he aching to hold her in his arms again, to lose himself in the wonder of that moment? Ellie held her breath and lifted her eyes to meet his.

What she saw made the blood slow in her veins. As Amadeo stared at her there was not a hint of recognition in his eyes. She'd expected discretion, of course. They were in the middle of a meeting, after all. What she hadn't expected was the look of haughty disdain that he now fixed on her.

"Miss Goldwell will deliver," he said coolly. "I expect nothing less." He was repeating what the creative director had said but, coming from him, the declaration sounded nothing like Vera's vote of confidence. The way he said the words, so clipped and cold, made it clear that this was an order.

With those words he was making a statement, loud and clear, but one that only Ellie would understand. The kiss had meant nothing to Amadeo. He was making sure she knew that. Ellie had no doubt about that.

Even though she could feel the heat rise up her neck she did not drop her gaze. His frigid stare was confirmation of what she'd suspected. Amadeo had played her for a fool.

It would not happen again.

CHAPTER NINE

Eight days. That was how long Amadeo was away from his Buenos Aires office. Eight long days in which he'd pushed himself, attending meetings with his bankers, his research and development team in Cordoba, and then the site in Tucuman where he would build his next manufacturing plant.

His departure had been deliberate. That night he'd taken Ellie to dinner, that moment when his lips touched hers, he knew he'd lost the battle. Why in the world did he find it so hard to resist Ellie Goldwell?

But he had to, and that was why he'd pulled away, physically and emotionally. There was no way he was going down that road with her, not when she was now his employee.

Next day when he'd seen her in the meeting, he'd been careful to divest his gaze of any hint of emotion. He could not afford to send the wrong message – to Ellie or to anyone who might be scrutinizing the look that passed between them – no matter that what he'd wanted to do was march over, pull her up and into his arms, and kiss those honeydew lips again.

Amadeo gave a grunt of annoyance and turned the key in the ignition. He'd been daydreaming again and it annoyed the hell out of him. *Cristo!* He was a grown man, not a schoolboy.

Twenty minutes later, when he pulled up in front of his office building, he drew in a deep breath. He needed to clear his mind. He'd been away from the office for over a week and there was much to do. He had no time for distracting thoughts.

When he walked into the lobby the receptionist greeted him with a warm smile, a gesture which lifted his mood. When he got to his private office suite the welcome was not so warm. Instead of a smile, his executive assistant greeted him with a frown.

"Good morning, *Senor Castillo*. We have been trying to reach you all morning." Maria's look was grave.

"Why?" His question was brusque. He raised an eyebrow, waiting for her response. He was not used to his assistant questioning his whereabouts.

"I am sorry. Maybe your telephone was out of range." She shook her head, her frown replaced by a look of concern. "It is Ellie Goldwell, our model. There is a problem."

Amadeo frowned. "What kind of problem?"

"There has been an accident. We will have to rush her back to-"

"An accident? What happened? Is she all right?" Amadeo's heart thumped hard in his chest as he stepped away from where he'd been standing at Maria's door. He marched into her office, right up to her desk, not even bothering to hide his concern. "Where is she?"

Maria raised her eyebrows. She was probably surprised at his reaction. He didn't care. Quickly, she got up and went toward him. "It is okay, *senor*. The accident, it was not with her. She is fine."

Now Amadeo was even more confused. "Then why did you say she had an accident?"

"No, not Ellie. It was her mother."

A wave of relief rushed in but, just as quickly, it ebbed away. Something had happened to someone Ellie loved. He could only imagine her distress. "Where is Ellie?" He had to go to her. Immediately.

"We got the news two hours ago," Maria said. "They were in the middle of a photo shoot in the downstairs studio. Right now Ellie is with Vera, in her office. I will go and get her right away."

"Yes. Right away." He was repeating what Maria just said but those were all the words he could find. His mind was too distracted, too full of thoughts of Ellie. She was thousands of miles from home at a time when her mother needed her. And it was his fault. "Get her, please. Take her straight to my office."

He strode away, out of Maria's office and toward his own, pulling out his cell phone as he went. He would call his pilot and make arrangements for his private jet to be ready. He would have Ellie by her mother's side in the fastest time possible.

But when he tapped on the cell phone screen nothing happened. He gave a grunt of irritation. The phone was dead. As usual, he'd been so busy he'd forgotten to charge the darned thing. No wonder Maria hadn't been able to reach him.

Amadeo stalked into his office and from there he called Gabriel. "Be on standby," he said to his pilot. "I will have to get further details but make sure the plane is ready to leave at a moment's notice."

"*Si, Senor*. Consider it done."

Amadeo was about to hang up the phone but then he paused. "Thank you," he said into the phone and then he returned the receiver to its cradle.

He was pacing the floor, his head down and his hands clasped behind his back, when there was a rap at his office door and it swung open. As Maria held the door open Ellie hurried into the room, her eyes wide and her cheeks flushed. She was obviously upset. "Amadeo, I need to go home. My mother-" Her voice broke off on a hiccup and she stopped in the middle of the room, looking like she was on the verge of tears.

"I know," he said, going to her. "Maria has told me. I will get you home right away." He was reaching for her when he remembered his assistant. She was still standing in the doorway. He gave her a curt nod. "Thank you, Maria. I will handle this from here."

The second the door closed, signaling that they were alone, Amadeo did as he'd intended. He reached out to place his hands on Ellie's shoulders. As he gazed down at her he saw that her lips were trembling. "Are you all right?"

Ellie swallowed then she raised troubled eyes to his. "I'm...fine. But my mother. I don't know..." As her voice trailed off she drew in a shaky breath.

Involuntarily, Amadeo's grip on her shoulders tightened. "What did you hear?"

"Somebody rear-ended her car. Thank goodness the kids weren't with her." She shook her head. "She was the one who called me. She said her injuries aren't too serious but I don't believe her." Her eyes widened. "She's in the hospital. That's where she called me from. If they checked her into the hospital it has to be serious." Again, her mouth trembled, but this time she bit down on her bottom lip to fight back tears.

At the sight of her, in such pain but still trying to be brave, his heart caved in. He'd resolved to leave emotion out of things as far as Ellie was concerned but to hell with it. Cold though he was, he could not bear to see her in tears.

"Do not cry, Ellie. You will be with your mother before the day is out. I will make sure of it. With you there, she will be fine."

As the words left his lips she lifted her head and looked up at him, her eyes searching his face as if for reassurance. "Do you really think she will be okay?"

"I'm sure of it," he said, knowing he would do anything in his power to make it so.

A soft sigh escaped her lips and then she gave him a tremulous smile. "Thank you," she whispered. "I needed that."

As she gazed up at him, her eyes so full of gratitude, it was too much for Amadeo. He'd been wanting to kiss her again, resisting it the whole time, but not anymore. Releasing her shoulders, he moved to cup her face in his hands. Then, as her eyes widened, her lips parting on a sigh, he dipped his head and captured her mouth with his own.

He was surprised, but pleasantly so, when Ellie responded hungrily. As her hands slid up his shoulders she went on tiptoe, all the better to meet his kiss, and for everything he gave she rewarded him with twice as much in return. Maybe it was the emotion of the moment that was driving her. She was clinging to him, melting into him, sighing for him, and Amadeo took full advantage of her ardor.

Releasing her face, he slid an arm behind her back and pulled her closer. Sliding his fingers into her hair, he tilted her back, forcing her to cling to him as they kissed. Now in total control he plundered her mouth, branding her with the passion of his kiss, making his desire plain as day.

With his kiss he gave her the gift of his strength, the power of his resolve to be there in her time of need. No words were necessary. His kiss would tell her all.

When he finally drew away, reluctantly ending their embrace, she was gazing up at him, eyes dark with emotion, her chest rising and falling as she caught her breath.

It was that look in her eyes that was his undoing. That look told him that whatever he was feeling, she was feeling it, too.

It was then that he knew that all was lost. Employee or not, he wanted Ellie Goldwell. He would not stop – he could not – until she was his.

After a kiss like the one they'd just shared the matter was out of his hands.

• • ❧ • •

AS SOON AS THE PLANE touched down on the runway Ellie fumbled at the seatbelt, ready to gather up her belongings.

"Just a moment, *senorita*. We must taxi to the gate. It won't be long." Cassandra, the attendant, had been solicitous throughout the whole journey and now she gave Ellie a gentle smile. "I know you are anxious but we will be there soon."

Ellie drew in her breath then she nodded. She knew the rules. She should remain seated until they were at the gate and the seatbelt lights were off. They just didn't seem to be getting to the gate fast enough. After rushing from the office then spending more than ten hours in the air she was exhausted but as soon as her feet touched solid earth she would be catching the first taxi she could find. There was nothing that could keep her away from her mother any longer.

But when the plane finally pulled in and she hopped up to get her bags, Cassandra hopped up, too. "I shall come with you," she said as she hurried toward the door. "There is a car waiting for you. I will take you to it."

"A car? I didn't reserve a car."

"Amadeo has arranged it. You will be taken directly to the hospital." She was unlocking the door as she spoke. As soon as it was open she beckoned to Ellie. "Let us go. I know you do not want to lose a moment."

Cassandra was true to her word. She grabbed the larger of Ellie's bags and preceded her into the airport terminal then steered her to a special line where she bypassed the crowd and was checked through immigration in less than ten minutes.

And then they were off, streaking through the airport until they flew through the sliding glass doors that opened onto the sidewalk. As soon as they stepped outside, Cassandra punched a number into her phone. "We're here. Aisle 3B. You can come around now."

To Ellie's chagrin, it was a stretch limo that pulled up in front of them. People were turning curious stares their way. Model though she was, she hated being the center of attention. But then there was no time to worry about it. Cassandra was pulling the door to the limousine open.

"Goodbye, Ellie. It was good meeting you." The attendant held out her bag and as she took it, Cassandra gave her a quick hug. "I hope all will be well with your mother," she whispered.

Ellie felt a lump in her throat. Everyone – Cassandra, the pilot and even Amadeo – was being so kind. She would forever be grateful. "Thank you," she said, her voice thick with emotion. "Thank you for everything."

After that, the driver moved swiftly and within twenty minutes he was pulling up in front of Lincoln Hospital. Before he could even come around to help her, Ellie was out of the car, bags in hand. "Thank you." She waved to him, smiling her thanks, and then she turned and hurried into the reception area. By this time it was after eleven o'clock at night but all her tiredness had fled. All she wanted was to see her mother.

It was the hospital volunteer who escorted her to the third floor. There, she found Abby lying in a hospital bed in a dimly lit room, the white bed sheet drawn up to her chest, her eyes closed. At the sight, Ellie's heart lurched. Was she unconscious?

She deposited both her bags on the chair by the door then quickly crept toward the bed. Although there was not much light in the room she could see her mother's face, relaxed and peaceful, and a ripple of relief ran through her. Abby couldn't be unconscious and look so peaceful, could she?

Desperate for reassurance, Ellie reached down and took the hand that peeked out from under the covers. She needed to touch Abby, feel the blood pumping through her veins. She just wanted to know that her mother was all right.

Ellie wrapped both her hands around her mother's, feeling the familiar veins on the back of her hand, feeling its weight and its warmth. She was gazing down at that beloved hand, stroking the back of it, when the fingers flexed then curled around hers.

Ellie's gaze flew to Abby's face. Her mother was gazing back at her, a gentle smile on her lips. "Mom, you're awake. You're...okay?" Ellie moved closer so she could see her mother's face, partially hidden in the shadowy room. "What happened?" Her words came out in a tearful whisper. Seeing her mother lying there, looking back at her, had all the emotions rushing right back.

"It's okay. I'll be all right." Abby's voice was hoarse but she was still smiling. She cleared her throat and tried again. "I got shook up, that's all. I'll be out of here in another day or two. Pull up a chair and rest your legs." She was lifting her chin as if to beckon toward the chair but she stopped mid-movement and winced. "Sorry. My neck is still sore."

"Don't move. Please stay still. I'll go get the chair." Ellie was away and back in seconds, pulling up the chair and taking her mother's hand again. "What happened, Mom? Are you badly hurt?"

Abby grimaced. "I ache all over but, thankfully, there's no serious injury. I got whiplash and I'll have to pay a few visits to the chiropractor but, outside of that, I'm good."

Ellie exhaled, releasing the breath she'd been holding. "I was scared, Mom. I'm so glad you're going to be all right." She was finally able to let her face relax into a smile.

But then her mother frowned. "Wait a minute. What are you doing here? Aren't you supposed to be in Argentina?"

"How could I stay when you'd been hurt? You called me from the hospital. There's no way I would be away from you, not when you need me."

"But when I called I didn't mean for you to come. It wasn't so bad that you had to leave your work." Abby was beginning to look upset. "Does this mean you lose your job?"

"No, I won't. At least, I don't think so. It was Amadeo who had me flown here in his private jet. He didn't even let me wait for a commercial flight."

Abby's face cleared. "So that's how you got here so fast. I just called you this morning." She glanced over at the clock on the bedside table. "It's still Friday, right?"

"We've got twenty-eight minutes before Friday ends."

Abby gave her a quizzical look. "So your boss flew you back to New York in his private jet? He went through a lot of expense to get you here."

Slowly, Ellie nodded. Those had been her thoughts exactly. "I know," she said softly. "He saw how upset I was and he knew how badly I wanted to be with you. He wanted to help." She paused as she thought about that. When she spoke again her voice was quiet. "I've got a lot to thank him for."

Abby squeezed her hand. "We both do. I'm glad you have a boss who's so thoughtful. I'm really happy you're here. I missed you, Ellie."

"Oh, Mom, I missed you, too." She was having a hard time keeping the tears in check but she did. She sniffed then leaned forward to give her mother a gentle kiss on the cheek. When she drew back she saw Abby blink and she knew her mother was as close to tears as she was.

Before they both started a cry-fest right there in the hospital room Ellie quickly changed the subject, asking the question that had been on her mind all day. "Where are the kids? Are they all right?"

"They're fine. Nancy was babysitting for me when I had the accident. She's spending the night at our place."

Ellie sighed her relief. "Thank God for Nancy. Always there when we need her."

"I know." Now it was Abby who was doing the hand squeezing. "We're going to be fine, Ellie. I'm not alone."

"No, you're not. I'm here now, and I'll be here until you're one hundred percent healed.

Abby smiled then squeezed her hand again. "We'll see."

Ellie knew what that meant. Healed or not, Abby was planning to shoo her back to Argentina as soon as she could, but Ellie had other plans. She wanted to see her mother well before she made any other move. As far as she was concerned, family came first.

She was opening her mouth, ready to tell Abby just that, when she heard her cell phone begin to buzz. She glanced at the clock. Eleven thirty-eight. She frowned. Who in the world could be ringing her so late at night, right when she was in the middle of catching up with her mother?

"Excuse me, Mom." Slightly peeved, she drew her hand from her mother's grasp and went over to the chair by the door. She was even more irritated when she pulled her phone from her bag and glanced at the screen. It was an unknown number. "Hello?" If the person on the other end of the line heard the annoyance in her voice she didn't really care.

"Hello, Ellie. How are you?"

At the sound of that voice, with its deep Spanish accent, Ellie drew in an involuntary breath. It was Amadeo. "I'm...I'm fine. Thank you for asking."

"And your mother? How is she?"

It surprised her but she actually thought she heard a hint of concern in his voice. "She's not too bad. Thanks." She drew in a steadying breath. "She'll have to do therapy for her back and take it slow while she recovers from whiplash. She should be out of the hospital in the next day or two, though."

"That's good. You must be relieved. With you by her side I'm sure she will recover even faster."

"Thanks to you, I'm here," she said. "Thank you for getting me here so quickly."

"You are very welcome. And do not worry about rushing back to do the project. I will put everything on hold until you are able to return." The words were said in Amadeo's usual clipped manner but she had the feeling he meant what he said.

"Thank you. You're very kind." She was careful to keep her tone as formal as his but inside she was jumping up and down. She'd assured her mother that she still had a job but she hadn't really been sure. Not until now. Now she would be able to dedicate her full attention to her family, knowing that she would still have a job at the end of it all.

After he'd wished her mother a speedy recovery then hung up, Ellie stood there by the door for several seconds more, lost in thought. For the life of her she could not figure Amadeo out. The man was an enigma, beast one moment and hero the next. And, on top of all that, he could be super-seductive.

The question was, which one was the real Amadeo?

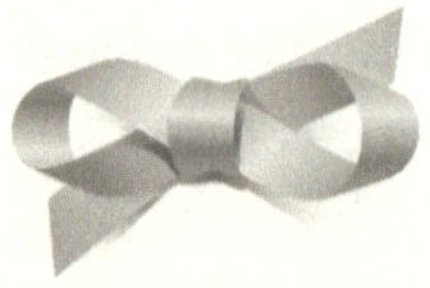

CHAPTER TEN

Amadeo slammed the car door shut with such force that if Mercedes-Benz Argentina could have seen his maltreatment of their SL65-AMG they would cringe. He was grumbling under his breath as he stalked away, heading toward the front door of his grandfather's estate house. It served as Rodrigo's home-cum-office. Even at the age of ninety he did not let a work day pass without heading into his office and checking on the operations of his four still very active corporations.

Amadeo still had his key to his former home so he let himself in but when he closed the door behind him he was not quite so vigorous as when he'd closed his car door. Then he headed across the wide and airy foyer and down the hallway toward the office. "*Abuelo*," he called out. "I'm here." There was no answer but that did not worry him. At his age, it was no surprise that his grandfather was becoming slightly hard of hearing. The real surprise was that his vision was as sharp as ever. He didn't even need glasses.

When he got to the office the door was ajar and he could see *Abuelo* Rodrigo standing by the windows that looked out onto the courtyard. His back was toward the office door, his hands clasped behind him. Amadeo grimaced, recognizing that stance. It was one that he often found himself using. His grandfather had rubbed off on him in more ways than one.

"*Buenos dias, Abuelo.* You wanted to see me?"

For a moment there was silence. His grandfather did not even turn to acknowledge his entrance. Finally, he spoke. "You are in a bad mood today. What is the problem?"

Amadeo walked over to stand beside his grandfather. He folded his arms as he turned toward the old man. "There is no problem," he said, "and I am not in a bad mood."

Rodrigo turned to look at Amadeo, his gray eyes piercing. "Do not lie to me. There is something pressing on your mind. You are not one to treat your possessions so shabbily."

So his grandfather had seen his arrival. Obviously, he'd been watching when Amadeo had taken his anger out on the car. He tightened his lips then drew in a breath, preparing to give Rodrigo an explanation that would end the discussion.

Before he could give his response, the old man spoke again. "It is a woman. That is the reason for your anger."

Amadeo's chin jerked up. Eyes narrowed, he glared at Rodrigo. The man was too astute for his own good. "Why do you say that?" he demanded. "I am a businessman. I have many things on my mind."

Rodrigo shook his head. "No. It is a woman. Problems with your business never make you want to destroy your car." His eyes narrowed. "And who is this woman who has my grandson acting in this manner?"

Amadeo's frown deepened. Even from he was a child he could never hide his emotions from his grandfather. Why did the old man have to be so darned perceptive? It was irritating, to say the least.

But, knowing Rodrigo would not stop until he got answers, Amadeo gave a grunt. "It is someone I have no business thinking about. She is an employee."

Rodrigo gave him a knowing look. "It is that model. The new face of Cosmeticos Aurora. She is the cause of your anger."

Amadeo glared back at him. Was there nothing the old man could not figure out? Expelling his breath, he released his arms and shoved his hands into his pockets then, muttering, he walked away. When he got to the sofa against the far wall he dropped down onto it. Annoyed with Rodrigo, but even more so with himself, he flopped back against the cushions, muttered a curse then raised a hand to rake his fingers through his hair.

"*Si?* What is that you were saying? I did not hear you." Rodrigo had turned away from the window to face Amadeo. Stubborn mule that he was, he would not let his grandson escape his interrogation.

"I said, yes, it is the model. She is the one who has me on edge." He said the words through clenched teeth. "Now you know. Are you happy?"

Rodrigo chuckled. "That is not the question. The question is, why are you not happy? You are attracted to a very beautiful woman. What is so strange about that?"

Amadeo slapped his hand down onto the seat beside him. "It is wrong, *Abuelo*. You know that. I do not mix personal feelings with business. And she is..." He stopped. He'd already said too much. It was none of his grandfather's business, what he was feeling. It was his cross to bear.

The fact was, it had been two and a half weeks since Ellie had left for New York to help her family while her mother recovered. Amadeo's life was so hectic that he should not have even noticed her absence. But he did. With every day that passed he expected his phone to ring, expected her to call to tell him she was ready to come back to Argentina. But his phone did not ring. Instead, she had sent him an e-mail, thanking him for allowing her time off. The following week she'd sent him a second email to advise that her mother was on the road to recovery. Since the new week started he'd heard nothing.

And the longer the silence stretched on, the more the tension grew inside him. The project was on hold while Ellie was away but that wasn't what was driving him crazy. The sad truth was, he was missing that contrary model of his, and he was having a hard time accepting that fact.

Because, how do you miss someone you hardly even knew?

But the thing was, he knew her. After tasting her lips, not once but twice, Amadeo knew all that he would ever need to know. And what he knew was that he wanted Ellie now more than ever before.

But Rodrigo didn't need to know that. It was time to change the subject. "You said you wanted to discuss some business," Amadeo said. "Well, I'm here now so let's get started. What business did you want to talk about?"

"Julio will be flying into Buenos Aires next week," Rodrigo said. "He is paying me a visit before he goes away to study." Slowly, he walked over to the chair by his desk then sank down into it. "I'm planning a surprise party for him. I want you to help me with it."

Amadeo cocked an eyebrow at him. "That is what you called me here for? You have assistants who are better able to handle this than I am. What do I know about party planning?"

"You will work with them. Supervise them." Rodrigo gave him a look that said he would not take 'no' for an answer. "This will be special, Amadeo. In case you have forgotten, I am ninety years old. Once this boy goes away I may never have the chance to see him again."

Amadeo could not help laughing. "You will live to be a hundred, maybe more. You're too busy running companies to sign off now."

Rodrigo laughed back. "Thank you for your vote of confidence. Still, I want you to do this for me, just in case."

Amadeo sat forward on the couch. "I will do anything you ask, *Abuelo*. You know that."

Rodrigo gave him a satisfied smile. "Yes, I know that. And there is one more thing I will have you do."

"What is that?"

"That woman who is turning you inside out, that model of yours, you must take her to the party with you."

Amadeo's frown returned. "Why should I do that?"

Rodrigo shrugged. "Because I want you to. Indulge me." His smile deepened. "I am an old man. We do not know how much longer I will be around."

Amadeo could only shake his head. Trust Rodrigo to play that card. He was not afraid to use it on his grandsons when he wanted his way.

Amadeo decided to give in to his demand. "As long as she's back in Buenos Aires by then, I will bring her."

"Good."

And maybe it was, indeed, good. When he saw Ellie again, meeting her in a setting outside of the office might be the best thing that could happen.

That way, he could taste her again, maybe even take things to another level. That way he could get her out of his system.

For good.

. . ❧ . .

"NO, NO, NO. NO LIFTING. Remember your back." Ellie rushed forward to get the grocery bags out of the car trunk before Abby could reach for them. She'd left the children back in the apartment with Nancy and had come to meet her mother in the parking garage.

"You are such a worry wart. I'm fine. My back doesn't hurt anymore." As Ellie stepped back, grocery bags in hand, Abby closed the trunk then put a hand on one hip as she turned toward her daughter. "Will you stop babying me?"

As they turned to walk, side by side, toward the entrance, Ellie shook her head. "No, I won't stop. You're forgetting that you're still in the recovery phase. You might feel better but you mustn't push it. I don't want you exerting yourself."

Abby gave an exaggerated sigh. "All right. I'll take it slow. I promise." Then she reached out to put a hand on Ellie's arm, bringing her to a halt. "As long as you promise to pack up and head back to Argentina. You can't stay with me forever, Ellie. You have to get back to your job."

"But Amadeo said I could stay as long as I need to."

"Exactly." Abby gave her a pointed look. "He said, as long as you need to. You don't need to."

Ellie grimaced. "But-"

"But, nothing." Abby turned away and walked up to the back entrance to the building. "Your boss has been extremely generous. Let's not take advantage of his kindness."

Ellie winced. Her mother had a point. Things seemed like they were back to normal so there was no reason why she should linger...except that, with her conflicting emotions, it was so much easier to hang out at home rather than face Amadeo again.

But how long could she hide?

They rode the elevator and as soon as Abby opened the door to their apartment they heard a yell. "Mama." Kevin came barreling toward the door, bumping Ellie in the leg, almost knocking her over.

Nancy laughed and ran forward to scoop him up. "Get back here, you little monster. Your mommy isn't supposed to be lifting you, remember?"

Still holding the squirming boy, she stepped back. "Doctor Riley's office called. They said they need to reschedule Peter's next therapy session. Can you give them a call?"

"Thanks, Nancy. I will."

The young woman nodded then turned away with Kevin still in her arms. "Come on. Let's go play with choo-choo train." That got her a shout of glee and then they were off to the corner of the living room which served as the baby's play area.

Ellie headed to the kitchen with the grocery bags and Abby followed. As her mother settled onto a chair she began packing the grocery items into the refrigerator and the cupboards.

"Peter's therapy is going really well," Abby said, as she dropped her handbag onto a nearby chair. "I'm surprised. I thought he would have been bored with it by now. You know, going to the clinic twice a week, doing the same thing over and over again."

"How many sessions has he done so far?"

"We did number eight on Monday. Tomorrow will be number nine. Oh, wait. I have to give the clinic a call. Be right back."

Ellie was still smiling to herself long after her mother had departed. As she packed the cookies and the box of tea into the cupboard her thoughts were on Peter and the fact that, by the time his forty sessions were completed, he should be free of the plague of epilepsy.

Her mind was also filled with thoughts of Amadeo, the man who had made it possible. Before the day was out she would call to let him know she was ready to return.

At the thought of seeing him again, her heart skipped a beat. She couldn't deny her excitement. She was aching to see him again.

But the man paid her wages. That was more than enough reason to steer clear of him, at least where matters of the heart were concerned.

This attraction she felt for him, she had to fight it. She had to keep things on a professional level. It would not be good if her heart got involved.

Now she was muttering to herself as she shook her head. No, it would not be good at all.

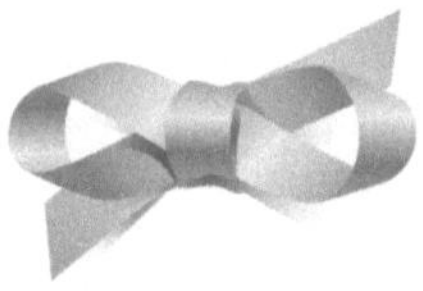

CHAPTER ELEVEN

The day Ellie returned to Buenos Aires Amadeo was out of town, meeting with the engineers and designers who would be handling the construction of the manufacturing plant. He planned to hold them to the highest standard, particularly where safety was concerned. That was why he hadn't left the meeting solely to his managers.

But even though he knew the importance of the meeting, even though he was the one who had chosen to be there, he spent the entire time wishing he could be somewhere else. As each hour of the day passed he was following Ellie on her journey back to Buenos Aires. When he'd gotten out of bed that morning, in his mind's eye he could see her arriving at the airport. By the time he pulled into the parking garage at the engineering firm he knew she would be in the air, on her way back to him.

When he realized where his mind had gone, Amadeo clenched his hand so hard the car key bit into his palm. Where had that thought come from? Ellie was on her way back to work. Why the hell was he inserting himself into that picture?

But even after that admission, that her return had nothing to do with him, he could not get her out of his mind. As the day progressed the thought that he would be seeing her soon was a major source of distraction.

"What do you think, *senor*. Is that option to your liking?"

At the sound of the head engineer's voice, Amadeo's glance jerked back toward him. "*Disculpeme.* I am sorry. I did not get that. Please outline the option again."

The man tilted his head to one side as he stared back at Amadeo. "Is everything all right, *senor*? You seem to have much on your mind." He raised his eyebrows. "Would you like to postpone the meeting?"

"No. Proceed with your explanation of the option. You will have my response." Amadeo's tone was stern and all business. The last thing he wanted was for the engineering team to think that his mind was not on the project at hand. He had to get Ellie off his brain. He reached for his glass of water and took a sip. When he returned the glass to the table he was ready. He nodded to the man who stood at the front of the room. "Continue."

When the day finally ended and he was able to climb back into his car, Amadeo gave a sigh of relief. It had been torture, pretending to be focused on technical drawings and construction budgets, when the whole time he was thinking about Ellie.

Dios. What the blazes had she done to him? He was acting like a love-sick boy, over a woman who'd done nothing but defy him from day one. She could not be human, this woman who had cast a confounding spell over him. Ellie Goldwell had to be a witch to have such power over him.

Amadeo laughed to himself as he drove back to Buenos Aires but it was a rueful laugh. Like Rodrigo said, Ellie had him turned inside out and she'd done it without even trying.

Next morning he went into the office even earlier than usual. He'd slept badly and when the clock finally touched five in the morning he got up. How could it make sense to lie there, staring at the ceiling? Besides, he had work to do.

So, after a forty-five minute jog around the estate, he grabbed some cereal, took a shower then headed into town. And there was another reason why he was going to the office so early. He would admit it to no-one but himself but he was anxious to see Ellie. *Dios*, he was pathetic.

When Amadeo walked into his office suite it was not yet seven o'clock. The place was deserted but he did not mind. He would get started on his work and he would have no distractions...except for his own darned wandering thoughts.

Sometime later there was a tap at his door and a smiling Maria peeked in. "*Buenos dias*. You are in very early today. May I bring you some coffee?"

Amadeo thought about that. "No," he said. "But thank you." He was high enough already, had been high ever since Ellie had called to say she was ready to come back. He definitely didn't need coffee to make things worse.

Maria smiled and was pulling the door closed when he stopped her. "Just a moment. As soon as Ellie arrives please send her to my office. I need to see...speak with her."

"Of course, *senor*." Maria nodded and pulled the door closed, leaving Amadeo to his work and his renegade thoughts.

An hour passed before he heard the second tap at his door. He looked up from the pile of papers on his desk. "*Entre*."

The door opened but this time there was no sign of Maria. The person who stepped in, eyes wide and a slight smile on her cutely pouting lips, was Ellie.

She closed the door behind her and slowly walked into the room. When she got to the middle she stopped and just stood there, staring at him with eyes like deep, dark pools of emotion.

It was like, whatever he'd been feeling, she'd been sharing it, too. There was no exchange of words between them. Right at that moment, the look they shared said it all. His chest tight with anticipation, Amadeo got up from behind his desk and began to walk toward her but before he'd made two steps she was moving toward him, too. Within seconds they were mere inches apart.

Now what?

Eyes narrowed, Amadeo scanned her upturned face. Had he read her right? If he made the wrong move it would be disaster.

But, no. The look in her eyes, the trembling of those lips, her swift intake of breath, told him all he needed to know. She wanted this just as badly as he did.

He made the first move. Reaching out, he touched her upper arm and when she leaned into his touch he lifted his other hand to grasp her shoulder.

Without hesitation, she tilted her face up toward him, her cheeks flushed and her lips trembling. The temptation was too great to resist. With a groan of defeat, Amadeo pulled her to him and when he lowered his head it was to capture her lips in a kiss that was almost brutal in its urgency. *Dios*, he'd waited so long for this.

And then she did something that confirmed she'd been hungry for this, too. Sliding her arms around his waist, she moved in even closer, molding her body to his, melting into his arms.

It was the license he needed to be assertive. Sliding his hand up, he tilted her face so he could have greater access to her lips. She did not resist.

Emboldened, he tightened his free arm around her then turned and as he kissed her breath away, forcing her to tighten her grip on him, he backed her toward the most private part of the room. Away from the windows, he let her sink down onto the sofa, never once loosening his grip or breaking the kiss.

When she slid her hand up his back, a moan escaping her lips, he knew it was time go further. He released her just long enough to tilt her back into the softness of the couch and then he was leaning over, but this time it was to slide his lips along the column of her neck. When she gasped as she arched toward him he smiled, his lips still gliding over her skin, and he slid lower down until he was grazing her collarbone.

Ellie sucked in a sharp breath and as he pressed his lips to her skin he could feel the pounding of her heart. She was breathing hard now, her breath coming in audible gasps, and the hands she'd slid up his arms were gripping him tightly, her fingers digging into his skin, making him all the more aware of how much her desire mirrored his.

Then, to his gratification, she released his arm and slid her hand into his hair, gripping the back of his head, pressing his face into her. She arched her back, giving him greater access to her body.

It was an invitation he gladly accepted. Sliding his lips lower, he was soon nuzzling the silky tops of her breasts, reveling in the sweet scent of her, reveling in her breathless reaction.

"Please, don't stop."

It was a desperate whisper that had him groaning in response. He was all too willing to oblige. He shifted on the sofa so he could slide down her body as he moved toward that succulent goal.

The phone rang. They both jumped.

Amadeo jerked his head up. "*Dios*. Not now." He raised himself up and away from Ellie just as she lifted a hand to her mouth, her eyes wide.

The phone rang two more times before he got to it. He grabbed the receiver and jammed it against his ear. "Yes."

"I'm sorry to disturb you, *senor*, but I have *Senor* Usher from the New York office on the line. Shall I put him through?"

"No, tell him I will...call him back." Amadeo put the receiver away from his face as he drew in a steadying breath. "I'll speak with him in fifteen minutes."

"Very well, *senor*. I will let him know that."

As Amadeo returned the receiver to its cradle he could only hope that Maria hadn't noticed that he'd been out of breath. The last thing he needed was to be the latest juicy tidbit on the office grapevine.

He drew in another breath then looked over at Ellie, knowing that there was no way they could pick up where they'd left off. Not right now, anyway. The sad fact was, they were in his office, possibly the worst place they could have chosen to fall into each other's arms.

He shook his head then gave her a smile of regret that their embrace had ended so suddenly. "This time I will not apologize for stealing a kiss."

Ellie's chest was rising and falling as she, too, fought to catch her breath but, to his relief, there was a cheeky grin on her lips. "That's all right," she said, her voice breathless. "No apologies necessary."

On hearing her words, Amadeo's heart quickened. It was the perfect response. Clearly, Ellie was not the 'fragile maiden' type.

And, for what he had planned, it was the perfect scenario.

· · ❧ · ·

ELLIE COULD NOT BELIEVE it. Amadeo had invited her to a party at his grandfather's house and she'd said yes. Just like that. No hesitation, no questions, nothing. Just – yes.

But after that mind-blowing kiss, how could she have said otherwise? Or the better question was, why would she even want to say otherwise? It was no secret, not to him nor to her. Boss or no boss, she was hopelessly attracted to Amadeo and if his kiss was anything to go by, it looked like he was feeling the attraction, too.

But how in the world they'd ended up on this road, she could hardly explain. It had been so sudden. Sure, they'd shared a kiss and then another, but the second time it was because she'd been so distraught. He'd only been trying to comfort her. But now this. This morning's kiss had been far more passionate and definitely more risqué than any before. And it had occurred even after she'd resolved never to let it happen again.

Ellie curled up on the sofa in her hotel suite, absently twisting a lock of hair around her index finger as she stared, unseeing, at the television screen. She could not stop thinking about Amadeo and how, despite her initial dislike for him, he'd become a temptation she could not resist. He was like a magnet with a pull so strong she could not keep from slamming into him.

Maybe it was a good thing that she was scheduled to be on the road with the creative team for the rest of the week. Being in the office with Amadeo, seeing him yet not being able to touch him, would be sheer torture.

But that night, as her head touched the pillow, Ellie knew she'd be counting the days until the weekend, until the party, until the time she would be with Amadeo again.

CHAPTER TWELVE

"**S**o this is Ellie Goldwell. I have heard much about you. *Mucho gusto en conocerle.* I am pleased to meet you, *senorita.*" The gray-haired man bowed gallantly then took her hand and gave it a soft kiss. When he straightened and looked back at her, he was smiling. "I am Rodrigo Castillo, Amadeo's grandfather, the one you should blame if he seems a bit rough around the edges. I am ashamed to admit it but I was a bad example for the boy when he was growing up." The glint in his eyes told Ellie he was not ashamed at all. In fact, as he spoke about his grandson what she saw was an unmistakable look of pride. "Welcome to *Hacienda Castillo.*"

"Thank you. I'm happy to be here." She almost felt like she should do a curtsy. This stately man, the grandeur of his home, the whole atmosphere breathed old world charm. It was like she'd entered another world, one where she would find castles and princes and knights in shining armor.

Amadeo, who had been waiting patiently by her side, inclined his head toward the hallway. "Shall we go? I would like to introduce you to the rest of the family."

"Of course." She nodded then gave the family patriarch another smile. "I'm sure I'll have the pleasure of seeing you again later."

"You most certainly will, *senorita*. I will not let Amadeo keep you to himself." He was still chuckling as she laid a hand on Amadeo's arm and they set off down the hallway.

When they got to the suite, which she could only describe as a grand ballroom, the party looked like it was well under way. The music of Tony Dize filled the space as he sang the hit song she'd been hearing ever since she got back to Argentina. *'Prometo Olvidarte'* translated to "I promise to forget you", a strange statement, but a song with such an upbeat rhythm that you couldn't help but rock to it.

But, at that moment, the music wasn't what was top of mind. Instead, Ellie's focus was on the number of people milling about the room, some dancing, some chatting, some lounging on comfortable seats against the wall, drinks in hand. She'd agreed to come to the party but she hadn't thought it would be this big. Somehow, when Amadeo had described it as a family gathering, she'd expected a dozen persons or so. This looked like twice that many, or more. She swallowed and, ever so slightly, her grip on his arm tightened.

He must have felt it because he looked down at her. "Everything all right?" When she nodded he turned his gaze back to the room full of people. "I've got a large family," he said. "Lots of cousins and uncles and aunts. *Abuelo* loves it when we all get together." Then he looked back at her and grinned. "They may look scary but they're not so bad when you get to know them."

It was his teasing grin that did the trick, releasing the tension within her, making her smile back. When he took her hand and headed for the far end of the room she was ready.

A tall, dark-haired man was leaning against the bar, his back to them. Amadeo reached out to tap him on the shoulder. When he turned, his smile widening as he laid eyes on Amadeo, Ellie immediately saw the family resemblance – the wide forehead, the square jaw and the firm, yet mobile, mouth. The eyes, though, were different. Where Amadeo's could go from the gray of granite to the smoky shade of rain clouds, his eyes were pools of liquid brown. And, just by the way he'd glanced from Amadeo and was looking at her, Ellie could tell he was a 'lady-killer'.

"Well, who do we have here?" he asked, his eyes trained on Ellie. "No, don't tell me. It must be the new face of Cosmeticos Aurora. I was told she is the most beautiful girl in the world."

His compliment was so sudden and so over-the-top that Ellie couldn't help but laugh. "And you must be Julio. Your reputation precedes you." On the way to the house, Amadeo had given her a quick rundown on his cousins and this one had stuck in her memory. He was the one Amadeo had warned her about. The inveterate charmer.

Amadeo didn't seem bothered by him at all. Obviously, he didn't take Julio seriously, because he only shook his head and gave his cousin a look that seemed to say, 'grow up, will you'?

"This is Ellie Goldwell," he said as he presented her. "Ellie, meet Julio, the cousin I told you about."

"I'm pleased to meet you, Julio. It's good to put a face to the name." Ellie raised her arm for a handshake but, like his grandfather, Julio put her hand to his lips and planted a soft kiss there. The way he did it, though, put his grandfather to shame. It was as if he were both greeting her and seducing her in that simple gesture.

"The pleasure is all mine, *Senorita* Ellie. I hope what Amadeo told you about me was all good."

Ellie chuckled. "Well, he did tell me you can be a charmer. He certainly wasn't lying."

"Ah, a compliment. Thank you, cousin." He gave Amadeo a huge grin.

Amadeo didn't respond to the comment and Ellie could not blame him. Being called a charmer might be a compliment in Julio's eyes but it could also be taken another way. Thankfully, Amadeo did not debate the point. He turned, and as his eyes scanned the room, he whistled. "They all came out, didn't they? Even *Tia* Elena."

Julio leaned back and propped his elbows on top of the bar. "You know she never misses an opportunity to gossip. With all these people here she won't run short of listening ears."

"Hmm." Amadeo gave an absentminded nod. "Where's Sergio? I thought he'd be here."

"He is. He's talking to Enrique and Miguel. They're over there." Julio jerked his chin toward the other end of the room where a knot of men congregated. "He was asking about you earlier."

"Yes, there's something I need to discuss with him before he does his usual disappearing act." He glanced down at Ellie. "Will you excuse me for a quick minute? Julio will take care of you till I get back."

"Of course," she told him. "Go right ahead. I'm a big girl."

He smiled at that and gave her a quick nod then he set off across the ballroom, greeting family members as he went.

"So. It's just you and me."

Ellie had been gazing at Amadeo's disappearing back but now she turned toward Julio. She found him looking back at her, a smug grin on his lips. "So tell me about Ellie Goldwell," he said. "I'm dying to get to know her."

Obviously, he was trying to turn up the charm. He was a Casanova, all right, and he was handsome enough to turn the head of any woman. Just not her. He couldn't have known this, of course, but her interest was in a man Julio probably thought meant nothing to her except for being the source of her income. He could not know that she'd come to the party hoping that, before the night ended, Amadeo would kiss her again.

"I'm afraid Ellie Goldwell is a mystery," she said, teasing him. "Sometimes easygoing and sometimes a wicked witch." She was trying to warn him, in a most subtle way, not to mess with her. He seemed a nice guy and he was Amadeo's cousin. She wouldn't want to have to slam him at the expense of his obviously huge ego.

Julio only laughed. "May I offer you a drink?" he asked, changing the subject. "What would you like?"

"I'm not much of a drinker," she admitted. "Cranberry juice would be fine."

He gave her a slight bow. "Coming right up." He turned to speak to the uniformed young woman behind the bar.

With Julio's attention directed elsewhere Ellie took the opportunity to look back across the dance floor, her eyes in search of Amadeo. He'd moved from where she'd last seen him but he was one of the tallest men in the room so he shouldn't be hard to find. She let her gaze wander as she looked for a head of dark hair that would be towering above most of the others in the room.

"Don't search too hard. He went outside with Sergio."

Ellie turned back to find Julio gazing at her, the drink in his hand.

He gave her a questioning look. "You seem anxious to locate your boss. Scared to be alone with me?" Then, before she could answer, his gaze narrowed. "Or is there more to this than meets the eye?"

Ellie frowned. Julio was too discerning for his own good. Wanting to throw him off track, she laughed and shook her head. "I was just curious about where he'd turned, that's all."

"Good. You seem like a nice girl. I don't want you to fall victim to one of us Castillos, especially Amadeo." He grimaced then turned to pick up the bottle of beer the server had set on the counter beside him. "Use them then lose them," he muttered. "How's that for a rule to live by?"

"Excuse me?" Ellie frowned, not sure she'd heard all his mumbled words. "What did you say?"

Julio shook his head and took a swig of his beer then he looked at her. "Nothing," he said. "Forget I said anything."

"But what did you mean by that, use them then lose them? Were you talking about Amadeo?"

He flashed her a guilty look but then he shook his head again. "No," he said. "Not Amadeo. That was all about me." His lips twisted into a crooked smile. "I am a…" he paused, his brows crinkling, "…a cad. That is what you call it in English." He shrugged. "I am sorry. I am what I am."

Ellie could have slapped him. He really was a cad, to say such things. Annoyed, she was turning away when she saw, coming toward them, that head she'd been searching for. Amadeo was on his way over. Thank goodness for that.

It was when he got close that she realized he was accompanied by two other men, both of whom were smiling. Immediately that they came to stand in front of her Amadeo nodded toward the newcomers. "Ellie, I have a couple more cousins I'd like you to meet. This is Sergio." He pushed the younger of the two men forward. "He's been bugging me for introductions."

Sergio reached out to take her hand. "I have been dying to meet you, *senorita*. Now my night is complete. You are even more beautiful up close."

Ellie smiled. What was it with these Castillo men? Were they all charmers? Wasn't it an irony that the one she liked was the one who seemed the least interested in being charming? "Thank you, Sergio. You're very kind."

The second man stepped forward. "And I am Enrique, the only sane one in this bunch." He stuck his hand out and when she took it, his handshake was firm. She liked that.

"I'll hang with you, then," she said. "I like sane people."

They all laughed but Enrique took her seriously. Before anyone else had a chance to claim her, he gave her his arm. "Come with me," he said as he gave her an indulgent smile. "I want to show you off."

And so he did. Enrique took her all around the room, introducing her to aunt this and uncle that, and to myriads of cousins. She met his sister and his two brothers. She even got the chance to speak with *Abuelo* Rodrigo again.

"How is that grandson of mine treating you?" he asked.

"Enrique?" She glanced up at her escort. "He's a real gentleman."

"No, not this one. I am speaking of Amadeo."

That threw her off. "Oh. He's been treating me quite well, thank you."

"Good. If he ever steps out of line you call me, do you hear? I know he can be a bully at the office sometimes. *Un maton*." He shook his head and chuckled. "A real chip off the old block." He shifted his cane to his other hand. "Now it is time for me to get some rest. I am not as young as I used to be." Still chuckling, he turned to go. "*Buenas noches*, Ellie. Remember to call me."

"I will. Good night." Ellie smiled and waved her goodbye. Of course, she had no intention of calling *Senor* Castillo for any reason. Who ever heard of someone calling their boss's grandfather? For what? A chitchat? She didn't think so.

"He means it, you know."

Ellie looked up at Enrique. "Really?"

He nodded. "He wouldn't have said that if he didn't mean it." He gave her a lopsided grin. "He must really like you."

Having no answer to that, Ellie dropped her gaze. She was glad when someone tapped Enrique on the shoulder, distracting him for the moment.

"I'll take over from here."

Ellie's head jerked up. She would know that voice anywhere. It was Amadeo.

Enrique shook his head. "Can't have her out of your sight for too long, can you?" But his smile said he was teasing. He released her arm and stepped back. "I look forward to meeting you again, Ellie."

She returned his smile. "Likewise."

Even as Enrique retreated Amadeo did not glance in his direction. His eyes were only on Ellie which, to her chagrin, soon had the heat rising in her cheeks.

"Shall we dance?"

Relieved at the excuse to drop her gaze, Ellie nodded and took his hand so he could lead her to the spot that seemed to have been designated for those who cared to dance.

There, he turned to her. "Now you will see what a terrible dancer I am."

That made her laugh, easing the tension. "You'll be in good company. I'm not too good at dancing either."

It didn't take long for Ellie to realize that Amadeo had lied to her. Quite blatantly, in fact. The way he rocked to the music, his movements so fluid, told her he was a natural. That made her more than a little nervous. Would he laugh at her effort to follow, letting her body sway with his? Soon, though, it didn't matter. She was having so much fun dancing anything and everything, from the tango to hip-hop, that she forgot to be self-conscious. Who could be, when you were rocking to the beat of 'Bailando' by Enrique Iglesias, a catchy mix of latin pop and Jamaican dancehall reggae? She didn't even care that Amadeo was watching her with obvious amusement.

They'd been dancing almost forty minutes when he moved in close. He lowered his head and put his lips to her ear. "Let's get out of here," he whispered, and there was a hint of urgency in his tone which she did not miss.

"I'm right behind you," she whispered back.

Taking his hand, she followed him through the crowd toward the exit. Their only stop was to speak to Julio. Amadeo gave him a brotherly slap on the back. "Congratulations on the move, old man. Good luck with the studies."

"You're heading out now?" Julio glanced from him to Ellie. "Not staying for some grub? They're going to serve dinner soon."

"I'm afraid not. Please let *Abuelo* know we had to go."

Julio shrugged. "He turned in already. You know how it is when you hit ninety." He turned his gaze on Ellie. "I wish you could stay, though."

Amadeo's grip on her hand tightened. "Sorry, she can't." After that, he made quick work of the goodbyes and soon they were at his car and he was holding the door open for her.

Ellie could sense Amadeo's desire for her and, right then, she was more than willing to assuage it. She would be brave and invite him to her hotel suite. She did not want the evening to end. "When we get back to my hotel-" That was as far as she got.

"Who says we're going to your hotel?" He seemed amused. "We need privacy, discretion. I've got the perfect place."

He didn't tell her where this perfect place was, but as Ellie slid onto the passenger's seat she could feel her body tremble with anticipation.

CHAPTER THIRTEEN

Amadeo drove swiftly along Uruguay Street, his body so aware of Ellie sitting just inches away from him that he ached. He'd felt the tension since he laid eyes on her that evening but now he was suffering. He was hard as rock. He couldn't get her to his apartment fast enough.

When he finally drove onto the grounds of the apartment complex Ellie leaned forward to gaze up at the *Recoleta* apartment building. "Wow." The word came out in a reverent whisper. "This is beautiful."

He nodded. "I own a penthouse apartment here. It's got a private elevator so we won't have to worry about prying eyes."

She nodded but she didn't take her eyes off the building and the entrance. Even when he parked the car she still kept her gaze averted. Realizing she was probably nervous, he reached out and tapped her on the shoulder. "Hey, wake up. Don't fall asleep on me now." It was his attempt to lighten the mood.

She looked at him then, and shook her head. "I'm more awake than you are. See?"

She opened her eyes wide, making him laugh. That trick must have worked because she laughed back then turned and reached for the door handle.

"Hold on. I'll get that." He got out and went around to open the door for her. When she stepped out and looked up at him her gaze spoke volumes. She was ready.

No further words were necessary. He took her hand and it was small and soft and just a little bit moist. He could only hope it was because she was as anxious as he was, for what would come next.

He got his confirmation when they got to the penthouse floor. She preceded him into the apartment then he stepped inside and pulled the door shut behind him. And then, as he stared down at her, she walked right up to him and into his arms.

It was she who pushed the jacket off his shoulders then tilted her face up for his kiss. He didn't need a second invitation. Lowering his face to hers, he captured her lips in a hungry kiss that would leave her in no doubt about his state. He wanted her so much he ached.

When they finally drew apart they were both panting. "*Ven conmigo. Quiero ser contigo.*" Realizing he'd switched to Spanish, he shook his head and took her hand. "Come." That was all he said but he was sure she knew exactly what he meant as they crossed the living room and headed for the bedroom.

As soon as they slammed the door shut behind them, things fell apart. Like they'd been starving all night long they reached for each other, Ellie attacking the buttons on his shirt as he slipped her scarf off her shoulder. She was fast. In no time she had his shirt flapping open. He shrugged it off his shoulders, letting it fall to the floor, leaving his chest bare to her gaze.

Her eyes widened as she stared back at him and then she swallowed. Before she could grow nervous and change her mind, he bent and wrapped his arms around her legs then lifted her up his body so that her belly pressed against his lips. She was still clothed so he couldn't nuzzle her like he wanted to, but that would soon be corrected.

With her still raised high, her hands gripping his shoulders, he walked straight to the king-sized bed in the middle of the room then dropped her into the softness of the plush pillows. Immediately, he went to her, nuzzling her neck as he slipped the spaghetti straps from her shoulders. He moved away from her just long enough to slide the dress down her body and off her legs, leaving her lithe body bare to his gaze. Or almost. She was wearing black silk panties with matching bra and, as delicious and tempting as she looked, he wanted to see more.

He leaned over her, eager to release her breasts from their sexy silk covering, when she reached up and grabbed his shoulders, pulling him down so she could nuzzle his taut nipple. He groaned but then, wanting to be ready for her in every possible way, he scooped her up and turned with her in his arms.

She reached up to hold on to his shoulders. "Where are we going?"

He dipped his head to plant a kiss on her forehead. "I worked up quite a sweat on the dance floor," he said. "I want to be nice and clean," he gave her a wicked grin, "before I let you kiss me all over."

Ellie rewarded him with the most beautiful blush and made him laugh when she ducked her head and pressed her face into his shoulder.

"You *are* going to kiss me all over, aren't you?" he pressed. He wasn't surprised when she refused to answer but when she nipped his shoulder with her sharp teeth, he jumped.

"You naughty girl," he growled, "you're going to pay for that."

She let out a tiny squeal and clung to him, probably anticipating a dunking in the tub but, although she didn't know it, he had no intention of following through on his threat of revenge. At least, not in a way that she would mind.

Gently, he let her slide back down his body until she was standing on the bathroom rug. He bent his head to her ear. "I will undress you," he whispered, "but then you will undress me."

She drew in a shaky breath then lifted her hand to bite down on her index finger.

He chuckled. "Scared?"

She didn't look up but she immediately shook her head. "Never," she whispered and her tone was defiant, just like the old Ellie he'd come to know and l...

Amadeo caught himself just in time, just as he was about to think something inappropriate, something totally unexpected. *Gracias a Dios*, it was a good thing Ellie could not read minds.

Irritated with his slip of the tongue or, in this case, his slip of the mind, Amadeo distracted himself by moving quickly. He bent to lift Ellie again but this time when he crossed the spacious bathroom, passing the Jacuzzi hot tub on his way, he deposited her in the shower and stepped in behind. Then, with them still in undergarments he turned on the spray, letting the water cascade over their heated bodies, feeling it soak the fabric till it clung to them.

As he stood behind her, Amadeo reached around to cup Ellie's breasts in his hands, making her sigh. When he pinched her pert nipples her body stiffened and her sigh became a groan. It was time to turn up the heat.

He released her, but only to snap the bra open and slide the straps off her shoulders, letting her breasts fall free. Then, not giving her time to recover, he turned her to face him and dipped his head to capture a turgid nipple between his teeth.

"Mmm." The soft moan escaped her lips, providing perfect proof of her pleasure, the sound of it making his already hard member go rigid. He was getting close to breaking point.

Amadeo released her nipple but only to slide down her body, his thumbs hooked into the waistband of the slip of silk that hid her from view. As he slid it down her legs he could feel her tremble, telling him that she wanted this, telling him exactly what he wanted to hear. He planted a soft kiss at the top of her mound, making her tremble all the more. When he rose up to face her he took her hand in his. "Now it's your turn."

Although she'd seemed so eager just seconds before, now she blushed, but then she lifted her hand to wipe the water from her cheeks and gave him a shaky smile. She slid down his body and, like he'd done for her, she hooked her thumbs into the waistband of his shorts and pushed down, slowly then in one quick move, releasing his member to her gaze.

The only problem was, she was not looking at him at all. She'd ducked her head, letting the water soak her hair and her back, leaving him to stare down at her in amusement.

With a chuckle he reached for her, pulling her up so her face was level with his chest and, as the warm water ran in rivulets down their bodies, he slid his hands over the slick and silky softness of her breasts. When she sighed and moved in to suckle at his nipple he didn't stop her. It was what he'd craved all long.

She applied that same sweet caress to his other nipple and then it was his turn to make her moan. He reached down to cup her bottom in his hands and, like he'd done before, he raised her up but this time it was so the tips of her breasts hung like succulent strawberries at his lips. He partook of the fruit, sucking a nipple deep into his mouth, soothing it then worrying it until Ellie squirmed in his arms. When he switched to the other nipple she dug her fingers into his shoulders, her nails biting into his skin.

It was enough. He'd tasted her, savored her, and now it was time to consume her. Amadeo hit the faucet, cutting off the cleansing flow, then he took Ellie in his arms and strode back into the room where he laid her on the bed. They were still dripping wet but there was no time to do anything but satisfy the hunger. He lay on the bed beside her and, wanting to make sure she was totally ready for him, he imprisoned her lips. As he kissed her he let his hand wander down to that sweet spot between her legs. There, he stroked and caressed until she moaned into his mouth.

Satisfied, he released her, but his gaze never left her as he reached over to the nightstand with one hand and opened the top drawer. He felt around, knowing exactly what he needed, to turn this scene electric. Not feeling it right away, he pulled away from her and rolled over to look into the drawer. What he saw made him frown. The confounded drawer was empty. *Demonio!*

"Maldito condon. Donde estas?" Amadeo was muttering as he got off the bed to kneel in front of the nightstand. He

pushed his hand all the way in, checking if there was anything stuck at the back. Nothing. He got the same result when he tried the bottom drawer.

By this time Ellie had rolled onto her side and was staring at him with a look of consternation. "What's wrong?"

Defeated, he got up from the floor and climbed back onto the bed beside her. Disgusted with himself, he expelled his breath on a groan. "Condoms," he said through clenched teeth. "I don't have any."

For a moment there was silence and then she lay back against the pillows. "Oh."

That was all she said but it wasn't hard to figure out what she was feeling. She was just as disappointed as he was and, on top of that, she was probably annoyed as hell.

There was no way he could let the night end like this. He rolled toward her and reached out to push a damp tendril from her cheek. "It is okay, *chiquita*. I will not leave you hanging. This night I will make your body hum for me."

Her eyes widened but, giving her no further explanation, he slid down until his face was mere inches from the junction of her thighs. There he nested, pressing soft kisses against her mound until her legs parted on a sigh, giving him greater access.

As promised, Amadeo teased and caressed Ellie, finding that pleasure point that made her writhe with want. When he stroked her there he heard the soft purrs as they escaped her lips. He knew it would not be long.

Spurred on by her arousal he heightened his assault, sweetly stroking until he felt her fingers slide into his hair, gripping his head so there was no hope for escape. Not that he wanted to. He'd promised her rapture and bliss and he was determined to deliver.

He got his reward when Ellie stiffened. She gripped his hair tighter than before, her breath coming in short, quick gasps. Her body began to shake and that was when he knew she'd reached her crest.

Through it all, Amadeo never let up. Right at that moment it was all about Ellie. It was all about pushing her passion to its peak.

She threw her head back into the pillows and gave a tiny squeal, her body shuddering for several seconds. Then, as he ran a soothing hand over the softness of her belly, her body relaxed and she sagged back into the bed.

Several more seconds passed as Amadeo let Ellie regain her breath. It was only when he heard her let out a long, slow sigh that he moved. When he got to the head of the bed he reached for her and gently gathered her into his arms.

Cradling her on his shoulder, he tucked her head under his chin, making sure she could not see his face. If she could have seen it she would certainly be worried. It was grim, and for good reason.

The problem was, Amadeo's feelings toward Ellie had begun to change. He'd been attracted to her from day one but now, what he was feeling was much more than that.

Unlike any other woman before, Ellie was becoming important to him and that was not good.

If his heart ever got involved, it would not be good at all.

CHAPTER FOURTEEN

"Ellie, are you listening to me?"

"Excuse me. What?" Ellie blinked and turned to look at the wardrobe manager. "Did you say something?"

"Yes, I said something. I've been talking to you for the past minute and a half and all you've done is smile back with a faraway look in your eyes. It's like you're in dreamland." Sonia shook her head as she picked up a slinky purple dress from the table. "This is the one I was showing you. I wanted to get your opinion on the color. Do you like this one or do you prefer the gold?"

"The gold, please. I think the gold one would suit my coloring." Feeling guilty that she'd been so distracted, Ellie walked over to the table and began fingering the garment, feigning interest when she couldn't have cared less if they'd told her to model a canvas sack. Right at that moment, fashion and clothing were the last things on her mind. The thing that dominated her thoughts – or, put more accurately, the person – was Amadeo. The night before, the time she'd spent in his bed, had been pure ecstasy. She'd replayed those moments, second by second, in her head and each time she'd done so her heart had swollen with an emotion so strong she'd had to catch her breath. No wonder she couldn't concentrate on what Sonia was saying.

Maybe it was a good thing Amadeo was away this week. He'd told her he would have to be in Brazil to meet with the managers of his subsidiary there. If she was so distracted, with him over a thousand miles away, she couldn't imagine what she would be like with him in the office. Her lack of focus would put her in hot water with the design team, for sure.

Ellie ended up having a super-hectic week, with photo shoots taking her from Buenos Aires to Rosario to Mendoza. She didn't mind, though, because it helped to keep her from spending her every waking moment thinking about Amadeo. Of course, thoughts of him were in competition with thoughts of her family, but she made sure to call home every night. She knew they were all fine. Not so with Amadeo. Not once did she try calling him, even though she knew the number to his cell phone. Neither did he call her. Maybe it was better that way. She was growing way too attached.

At that thought, she smiled to herself. Who was she kidding? If her intention had been to keep her distance from Amadeo it was much too late for that. After the night they'd shared, there was no turning back...at least, as far as she was concerned. She could only hope Amadeo felt the same way.

That thought sobered her a bit and she threw herself into her work, not wanting to dwell on any negative possibilities. Her energy paid off because they finished the three photo shoots early enough where the team was able to head back to Buenos Aires by Thursday evening, one day earlier than scheduled.

She spent Friday at the office, going through the rough shots with the team, and she was pleased when they expressed their satisfaction with the quality of the photos they'd been able to produce.

"You are one photogenic girl." Vera was grinning as she flipped through the photos. "We're lucky to have you. Look at this one, Santiago."

"She makes the job so easy." The photographer nodded as he took the photo from her fingers. "And it doesn't hurt that she has acting experience."

Ellie frowned. "I never said I had acting experience."

Santiago raised his eyebrows. "Well, you certainly carry yourself as if you do. Now I'm even more impressed."

Embarrassed at the praise, she shook her head. "I just do what you ask me. Your excellent direction makes all the difference in the world."

Santiago laughed. "You know exactly what to say to make me feel good. Smart girl."

That afternoon, Ellie left work early but although there were several hours to go before the sun set she did not linger on the road, even after Maria told her about a free concert to be held in *Bosques de Palermo*, one of the largest and most beautiful parks in the city. She declined the invitation to hang out with Amadeo's assistant and chose, instead, to head back to her hotel. Amadeo would be back in town that evening and she wanted to be in when he called.

If he called.

As she rode the elevator up to her floor she leaned back against the wall and closed her eyes. She could not even contemplate Amadeo not calling. He had to. She'd been patient all week, awaiting his return. She could not wait another day.

Ellie spent the rest of her evening reading the novel she'd bought at the nearby bookstore, or pretending to, anyway. Her eyes skimmed the words but every ten minutes she would glance at the phone, willing it to ring. She was so distracted that she read the same page five times before she finally threw the book down with a hiss of frustration.

And then she glanced at the phone again. "Ring, will you?"

It ignored her.

After a quick meal in the hotel restaurant, she hurried back upstairs and immediately checked for messages. Nothing. Deflated, she flopped down onto the sofa. Instead of waiting for Amadeo to call, should she do the calling?

Immediately, she shook her head. Not a good idea. She definitely didn't want to come across as desperate.

And so, as the minutes and then the hours ticked by, Ellie lolled around the hotel suite. She turned on the television then she turned it off again. She went out onto the balcony but within ten minutes she was back inside. She didn't even bother picking up her book again. It was so darned frustrating, waiting for a phone call that might never come.

When the clock struck ten she gave up. She'd resolved to be strong but she hadn't expected to feel so desolate. Accepting defeat, Ellie dragged herself off to the bathroom. She needed to release her tension. That was the only way she would ever get some sleep.

She filled the Jacuzzi tub, climbed in and slid down into the comforting warmth of the bubbling water. With a sigh, she closed her eyes and leaned back to rest the back of her head against the lip. It had been a trying day, so wonderful at the start but so worrisome in the end. She couldn't wait to bring it to a close and lose herself in sleep.

Ellie laid there so long the water slowly went from warm to tepid to uncomfortably cool but still she lay there, feeling too lazy and too darned miserable to rise. By the time she got out she was sure she would be wrinkly but she was too depressed to care. She was having a really rotten night.

And then the phone rang.

Ellie's eyes flew open. She jerked upright, startled back to the present. It was the second ring that spurred her into action. She scrambled out of the tub, splashing water everywhere, and streaked into the bedroom. She dived across the bed to grab the phone. "Hello?"

"How are you, Ellie?"

At the sound of Amadeo's voice, a delicious thrill ran through her. "I'm fine. How are you?" The words tumbled out in a breathless rush.

"Tired." He sighed. "This has been a rough week. I'm glad it's over."

"Oh. I'm sorry."

"Don't be. I've come to the best part." When he paused, Ellie held her breath. "I want to see you, Ellie. As soon as possible."

She sucked in her breath, not daring to hope. "You're coming over? Tonight?"

She could have kicked herself when Amadeo chuckled into the phone. "No, not tonight, *mi querida*. It's already too late for that. But I'd like to see you tomorrow. I'd like you to have dinner with me. You will say yes, *si*?"

"Yes," she said, without hesitation. "I'd love to." Maybe she sounded a bit too eager but now was not the time to play coy. She'd been on tenterhooks all week, waiting for this call, waiting for the chance to see Amadeo again. She was only too happy to say yes.

"Perfect. I will pick you up at six, then. Dress comfortably."

That piqued her curiosity. "Where are we going?"

"It will be a surprise," he said, his tone mysterious. "Don't worry. It's nowhere fancy. Casual wear will be fine."

That made her even more curious. "Can't you give me a little hint?"

He laughed. "Patience, *querida*. You'll find out tomorrow. Now rest well until I see you."

Long after the phone call had ended Ellie laid there on the bed, totally naked, too lost in her world of daydreams to be in any hurry to get dressed. Amadeo had called and she would be seeing him in less than twenty-four hours. And, as far as she was concerned, the time couldn't fly fast enough.

Next evening found Ellie ready and waiting at five forty-five in the hotel lobby. Dressed in black silk pants and a lacy top, she could only hope she was casual enough for where Amadeo planned to take them for dinner. He'd said casual but she hadn't wanted to take that suggestion too far. She guessed jeans and cotton shirt would have been way out of place.

But when she saw Amadeo, excruciatingly handsome in jeans and a black T-shirt that displayed his well-cut frame, she laughed.

He smiled back. "What's so funny?"

She tilted her head as she gazed up into his eyes, her heart racing as he came closer. "I told myself jeans would be totally inappropriate but here you are." She took the opportunity to look him up and down. "In jeans."

Just like she'd done to him, Amadeo let his gaze drift over her, making her so aware of him that her nipples tightened in her top. She could only hope he didn't notice. "You chose the perfect outfit", he said. "You look stunning."

Feeling the color beginning to rise in her cheeks, Ellie dropped her gaze and cleared her throat. "I guess we'd better be going now. I'm all yours." The words had hardly left her mouth before she realized her blunder. I'm all yours? Could she have chosen a worse line?

To her relief, it seemed that Amadeo was too much of a gentleman to acknowledge that subtle, though unintentional, invitation. Saying not a word, he gave her his arm and they exited the hotel in companionable silence. Soon, they were on their way.

The car ride was over forty-five minutes but Ellie enjoyed the trip. Along the way Amadeo entertained her with tidbits from his childhood, making her realize that he'd been something of a rebel during his teen years.

"You were quite the handful," she said as she watched him drive. "How did your grandfather manage you?"

He shook his head. "I was a real trial but *Abuelo* was no pushover. He raised me with a firm hand. Tough love, they call it, but I'm grateful. It's made me the man I am today."

"And your father?" She didn't want to be nosy but his story begged the question.

"As I told you, Mama died when I was eleven," he said, his tone casual. Ellie was not deceived. The slight strain in his voice told her his mother had been dear to him, and still was. "After that, I had to grow up real fast. My father was...well, let us say he was not really a father. That is why *Abuelo* took me in. I will always be grateful to him." He paused then frowned. "I don't know if I ever told him that."

For a moment he seemed lost in thought. Ellie remained silent, waiting for him to speak again. When he didn't, she dared to ask, "Your father, where is he now?"

Amadeo grimaced. "Who knows? I only ever heard from him two times in the last five years, both times when he needed money to pay off gambling debts. That was his downfall. Gambling." He drew in his breath and let it out slowly. "Victim of that bloody curse." The last part was said in a voice so low that Ellie could hardly hear it.

"What was that about a curse?"

He shook his head. "Just a family thing. Nothing important." Then he gave her a tight smile. "But enough about me. Let's relax with some music." He flipped on the radio, filling the car with music, telling her that their conversation, at least as far as his family was concerned, was over.

Ellie fell quiet but when Amadeo finally pulled off the road and turned onto a driveway she perked up. They were approaching a magnificent mansion at the end of a tree-lined boulevard. With its grand pillars and majestic windows, it looked like a residence fit for royalty. "We're going to have dinner here?" She peered out as Amadeo pulled the car in front and switched off the engine. "Is this a restaurant or someone's home?" Secretly, she hoped it wasn't the latter. She was not in the mood for another of his family gatherings. She just wanted to spend the night with him. Alone.

"It's someone's home," he said, confirming her fear but, just as her spirit began to sink, he continued. "Mine."

Her eyes widened. "It's beautiful. A real work of art." She tore her gaze from his and looked back at the building. "We're going to have dinner here?"

"We are."

"Alone?"

"Alone."

She bit her lip. Had she said that last word out loud? Hoping to distract him from her gaffe, she kept talking. "That's good. I mean, so we can get a chance to talk some more. You can tell me more about your family."

He laughed softly then reached out to touch her cheek. "No, *chiquita*. Tonight it's all about you."

Ellie swallowed. It was what she wanted to hear but, silly girl that she was, she was also a little bit scared. What if she did something to mess up this wonderful night? At the thought, her palms grew moist. She drew in a shaky breath then forced a smile. "I look forward to it."

That seemed to satisfy Amadeo because he nodded then turned to open his car door. By the time he came around to her side she'd taken some quick, steadying breaths and was ready for anything. She hoped...

Amadeo offered his arm and as she took it he gave her a smile so seductive that her body responded involuntarily. Thank goodness he would never know that she'd grown moist. Down there.

And that was a real cause for concern. If Amadeo could turn her on with nothing but a simple smile she could just imagine what would happen if he decided to turn up the charm.

If he did, there was no way she'd be able to resist. But the real question was, did she even want to?

CHAPTER FIFTEEN

Ellie gasped with pleasure when, after a tour of his palatial home, Amadeo took her out to a back patio. There, underneath the stars, was a table decorated with roses and flickering candles in crystal jars.

"Dinner by candlelight? But how did you do this? When?" Ellie could not hide her surprise and delight.

"Not me. My housekeeper. She prepared this meal especially for us." When Ellie raised her eyebrows he smiled. "Don't worry. She has already left. We are all alone." He lowered his eyelids. "As I promised."

Ellie didn't have an answer for that. She was only too happy when Amadeo took her hand and led her to the table. After she was seated, he lifted the covers on the dishes laid out there. "They're still warm," she said as she touched the plate in front of her.

"Yes. We timed it perfectly." Amadeo looked so pleased with himself that Ellie had to smile.

When she started eating, though, the smile gave way to a moan of pleasure. "Mmm. This is so delicious. What do you call it?" She lifted another morsel onto her fork and put it to her mouth.

"That is *Locro*. This stew is popular throughout all of Argentina. I'm glad you like it."

"That's an understatement. I love it." Just to prove her point, Ellie licked her lips. Big mistake. Like she'd set off a chain reaction, Amadeo's eyes followed her and, to her surprise, he was licking his lips, too.

But that was not the problem. It was the way he was doing it, his tongue sliding slowly over his bottom lip, his eyes never leaving hers. That was her undoing.

He wanted her. He was making that very clear. And she wanted him, too.

As delicious as the meal was, she was glad when it was over. And, to her joy, Amadeo had another trick up his sleeve. She didn't even know when he got the chance to switch on an iPod dock – maybe he'd used a remote control device – but the evening air was suddenly filled with the silky sounds of John Legend's, "All of Me."

"Dance with me." Amadeo had already come to stand by her chair and he was holding his hand out, awaiting her response.

"I would love to." She placed her hand in his and rose to stand by him, so close she could smell the faint fragrance of his cologne. He pulled her close, so close that she could feel the warmth of his body, a sensation that made her tingle with awareness. And then, as Legend's mellow croons washed over them, he pulled her closer still, this time until their bodies touched.

A jolt ran through her. The shock of it made her lift her arms to cling to him for support and then she was leaning into him, sliding her arms around his waist, resting her cheek against his cotton-covered chest. It felt so natural, so right.

His arms locked around her, Amadeo rested his cheek against the top of her head and so they danced, song after song, until he swung her off her feet and up into his arms.

Ellie squealed and grabbed his shoulders. "What are you doing?"

"Shh. You should know me by now, *mi amor*. I will not hurt you. Just relax." As soon as she let her body melt against him, Amadeo turned with her in his arms and strode through the open patio door. Inside, he did not stop. He crossed the foyer then headed for the stairs which he climbed two at a time. When he got to the landing he did not pause.

With her face tucked into his shoulder, she could not see where he was going, but she felt when he turned to press his shoulder against a door, prodding it open. This, she guessed, would be his bedroom. The thought, the anticipation, made her cling even tighter.

It was only when Amadeo leaned over to gently lay her on the bed that Ellie finally released him and opened her eyes. What she saw in his made her heart flip over. His eyes had turned a smokey gray, leaving her in no doubt about the state of his arousal.

As if confirming what she was thinking, Amadeo dipped his head to capture her lips in a kiss that had her arching her back in ecstasy. She was reaching for him when he drew away but it was only to intensify his teasing. He slid his lips down her neck and over her collarbone and in one swift move he'd captured a silk-covered nipple in his mouth.

But he did not linger. With a groan he pulled back and reached down to pull the top up her belly. "I want to see you," he whispered. "Touch you. Taste you."

He was lifting the blouse up and over her breasts when she covered his hands with hers, stopping him mid-journey. "Wait," she gasped. "I have something." When he gave her a look that told her he had no idea what she meant she reached down. "It's in my pocket." She slid her hand inside the pocket of her silk trousers and pulled out a shiny packet. She held it up to his view. "I came prepared," she said, "just in case."

For a second he stared at the object in her hand then his look of confusion gave way to amusement. Chuckling, he shook his head then he took it from her and leaned forward to plant a quick kiss on the tip of her nose. "I'm prepared," he said, still smiling as he pulled back, "but thank you for the back-up plan."

That settled, he continued with the task he'd begun, divesting Ellie of top, bottom and everything else besides, leaving her naked to his gaze. "*Hermosa*," he whispered. "So beautiful."

She lowered her eyelids, averting her gaze from the intensity of his stare. Maybe it was a good thing because, at that moment, Amadeo raised up to pull his T-shirt over his head. He got up off the bed and she could hear when he pulled his trousers and pushed them down his legs. She did not look. Curious though she was, she still didn't steal a peek.

And then she heard the unmistakable sound of a packet ripping. She waited while he sheathed himself. When he climbed back onto the bed she drew in a slow breath, opened her eyes and forced a smile. Her heart was beating like a kettle drum but she had to play it cool. She tilted her face to kiss Amadeo on the chin then reached up to pull him closer.

His response was to feather kisses along her neck, trailing a path across her cheek and toward her lips. There, he covered her mouth with his, his caress at first gentle then insistent then so demanding it made her melt beneath him. And then, even as he imprisoned her mouth, she felt him nudge her legs apart then raise himself up over her.

Ellie clung to his shoulders, a frisson of fear running through her. She sucked in her breath and closed her eyes tight.

And then she felt as his manhood pressed against her. It was a sweet, searing pressure that made her moan.

Amadeo continued to plunder her mouth, stealing her breath away, and as he did he sank down into her, breaking through her resistance, making her stiffen and dig her fingers into his back.

He froze, but it was too late. He was in, and although she felt imprisoned by his weight, impaled and unable to move, she wanted more.

Ellie pulled her lips from his but only to whisper, "Please. Don't stop."

"Ellie." His reply was a tortured groan. "Why didn't you tell me?"

He made as if to rise but she reached out and wrapped her arms around him. Afraid that he would leave her, she clung to him like she would never let go. "I want you," she sobbed, "more than anything."

He groaned again. "Are you sure?"

"Yes. Please. Give me all of you."

It was a desperate plea that finally seemed to get through to him. He pressed his face into the pillow, right by her head, and exhaled. And then he began to move, slowly, tentatively but as she began to move with him he gradually picked up pace.

Ellie matched him stroke for stroke, mimicking his moves, holding nothing back. He was gentle, oh so gentle, and so in control. He played her like a musical instrument, tuning her body to his until they moved in a seamless symphony, now slow and steady then with a quickening pace until the rhythm of their timeless tango took them to the brink and beyond.

A tremor shook Ellie's body and the shock of it, the sheer ecstasy and thrill, had her arching her back again, involuntarily, as her body sought to capture all that he had to give. A blissful sob escaped her lips as her body received him, caressed him, massaged him until he stiffened then uttered a guttural groan and slumped, breathless, over her.

Ellie lay there, cradling Amadeo to her as she listened to his panting, and that was when she knew, without a doubt, that she'd fallen hopelessly in love...

...and it was the most wonderful feeling in the world.

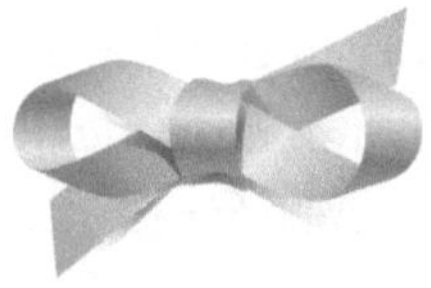

CHAPTER SIXTEEN

Mierda. It was one o'clock in the morning and still Amadeo sat there on the cold, hard stones of the patio floor, staring out at the shadows of night. He dropped his face in his hands and groaned. *Que tonto!* How could he have been such a fool?

He'd dropped Ellie back at the hotel and throughout the entire journey he'd tried to look cheerful. She'd seemed so blissfully happy that he'd done everything in his power not to dampen her mood. And so he smiled, and as he drove he reached out and touched her hand, and when she slipped into slumber by his side he drew her scarf around her shoulders.

At the hotel he'd held her close but he hadn't kissed her goodbye. She'd accepted his embrace without demur and had given him a tremulous smile when she'd turned to go. And all the while he was feeling like a jerk.

He'd come right back home and flopped down on the patio, that same patio where they'd danced. There, he'd chastised himself for what he'd done. He'd deflowered a virgin. How could he have been so stupid not to know?

He frowned, even as he thought about it. Ellie had always been so bold, so outspoken. Somehow, he had taken that to mean she was worldly, well experienced in the matters of life. Including sex. *Cielos!* He had been so wrong.

And now, knowing she'd been an innocent, all he could feel was disgust for himself.

What made it worse was the fact that he was her employer. What if she'd felt coerced into this because he was in a position of greater power?

It was a bit late to be thinking of that but there it was, another reason why he deserved whatever condemnation she threw in his direction. And she would do just that. He had no doubt there. And who could blame her?

Amadeo groaned and raked his fingers through his hair. There was one more thing, one more reason why he should never have gone down this road with Ellie. It was that bloody curse, the reason he'd resolved never to lose his heart to any woman. Use them then lose them, he'd always said, and he'd followed that rule to the letter.

Until now...

Even if he'd wanted to have his fun with Ellie and then move on, as he'd done with so many women before, how could he do that now? It was different with the other women. With some, there had been an understanding. With others, he'd simply been a scoundrel. But with Ellie?

How do you walk away from someone who trusted you enough to give you such a special gift?

• • ❧ • •

ELLIE WAS IN HEAVEN. She'd had no idea that love, and the lovemaking that came with it, could feel so good. She'd thought that night she'd gone to Amadeo's apartment had been the ultimate but nothing could compare to last night. Not when, so gently and expertly, he had made a real woman of her.

She let out a satisfied sigh as she stepped out of the shower and reached for the towel on the nearby rack. It was Saturday, the first full day of the weekend, and she was looking forward to spending it with Amadeo.

He hadn't said he would spend the day with her. Not yet, anyway. But she was expecting it. After the magical moment they'd shared the night before, she was dying to see him again. And the way he'd touched her, the way he'd gazed into her eyes, she was sure he felt the same way, too.

So, even though she'd had such an eventful night, one she would never forget, Ellie got an early start on her Saturday, rising just after dawn and having breakfast in the suite just so she wouldn't miss Amadeo's call.

He didn't call, not even after she'd finished breakfast and had hung around her hotel suite until almost noon. She didn't worry too much about it, though. He was probably exhausted and decided to sleep in late.

But then the hours ticked around to three and then four and still there was no call. She'd hesitated to do the calling, thinking it was couples' protocol for the man to call first, but she'd been waiting far too long. All day, in fact. When was he going to call?

When the clock snapped to the hour of five, Ellie had had enough. She would not wait a minute more. Where was he?

Worried now, she picked up the phone and dialed his number. It rang, and rang some more, and then it went to voicemail. She did not leave a message.

What in the world was going on?

Ellie waited one more hour and then she called again. Still only a voicemail recording. This time she decided to speak.

"Amadeo, I...I just wanted to know that you're fine. Could you call me, please? It's Ellie." That done, she ended the call and settled back to wait. And wait. And wait.

Right up to nine o'clock that night she waited. When the day ended with no return call from Amadeo she knew it wasn't going to happen. Clearly, he had no intention of calling her.

And with this realization Ellie climbed into bed, depressed. Devastated. And alone.

CHAPTER SEVENTEEN

"I can't do it, Julio. I can't do that to her."

"What are you talking about? You do it all the time."

"Yes, but this girl is...different."

Julio turned to look at Amadeo, the amusement plain on his face. "Going soft? The big, bad Amadeo Castillo is hesitant about hurting someone's feelings?"

Amadeo shoved his hands into his pockets and kicked the leg of the sofa. Hearing it from Julio, the confirmation that he'd always been a royal jerk, made things seem even worse. How do you go from that to playing nice guy?

"I'm glad you're thinking twice about hurting her, though. She seems like a nice girl," Julio's eyes narrowed, "one who works for you, one who I had no idea you were pursuing."

Amadeo frowned. "I wasn't. At least, that was not my intention...at first."

"Hmm." Julio looked like he didn't believe a word of it.

Amadeo didn't give a damn. He was telling the truth, about not intending to cross the line and about now not wanting to hurt her, and that was why he was going to nip this thing in the bud. He had to, before it developed into something neither one of them could handle.

"I'm going to do what I have to do to make sure she stays safe." More decisive now, he nodded in confirmation and sat on the arm of the sofa. "You know what I have to do."

Julio gave a snort. "You're still worried about that Castillo curse business? And you're going to let that stop you from moving forward with your relationship?"

"Enough. I already told you, there is no relationship. Ellie deserves better than what I have to offer." Irritated with Julio's line of questioning, Amadeo got up, the tension coiled too tight for him to remain in that position. He straightened and folded his arms across his chest. "She deserves a man who can give her unconditional love without a ton of baggage dragging behind. That's why I left a message on her cell phone, telling her I'd be away again. For a week. That will give her the time and the space she needs to regain perspective. While I'm away she'll think things through. She will realize that it's for the best."

"You didn't talk to her?"

"I tried. I only got her voicemail. I guess eight-thirty was too early to call on a Sunday morning." He dropped his arms and walked away from the sofa to pace the library floor. Than he stopped. When he looked back at Julio he was scowling. "I don't know why I'm telling you all of this. I must be going soft in the head."

Julio chuckled. "Or maybe it's the first time you've had your head in a muddle over a woman. So what do you do? You turn to your favorite cousin. Me." He was grinning now, which only served to irritate Amadeo more.

He shook his head, trying to clear his mind. Julio was right. This was the first time he'd ever been uncertain about a woman, wanting her like a parched man in the desert, yet wanting to keep her at a distance...for her own good.

He heaved a sigh. "You know I can't bring her into this, Julio. I'm a Castillo. I'm no good for her."

"It doesn't have to happen to you. Forget the damn curse." Julio's grin disappeared and now his look was grave. "We can beat this."

Amadeo tightened his lips. He shook his head, not daring to believe it. How could he take that risk when a sweet innocent like Ellie was involved? "We end up hurting all our women, Julio. I can't let that happen to Ellie. She deserves better."

"Just because your father-"

"My father has nothing to do with it."

"Stop denying it. He has everything to do with your decision." Julio glared at him. "Okay, so we're a family of gamblers. Some of us gamble with our money, some with our women. We even gamble with our lives. Some of us have fallen victim to that affliction but others have overcome and triumphed. Look at *Abuelo*."

Amadeo gave a snort. "*Abuelo*? He paid the ultimate price. He had to give up the woman he loved."

"But that does not have to be your fate-"

"Enough." Amadeo chopped his hand down, cutting off the flow of Julio's words. "I will leave for New York. First thing tomorrow."

"And Ellie?"

"There is still much work to do in Argentina. She will be occupied with the creative team. She got my message. She knows I will be away. I will call her after a day or two, when she will be ready to hear what I have to say."

Julio shook his head. "She's going to hate you."

Amadeo shrugged. "It is a price I will have to pay. It is for the best if she does not get her heart involved with me."

Julio raised his eyebrows. "Maybe her heart already is."

He did not reply. Julio was not telling him something he did not already know. All he could do was repeat what he knew in his heart. "I don't want to hurt her. I would rather deny myself than have her tie her hopes to a man whose demons will not let him go. There are better men out there. She will find one."

The look Julio gave him said he did not agree. "You're making a mistake."

Amadeo's response was a soft grunt. He turned away from his cousin and stared out at the gardens of his estate, knowing that he could not do otherwise, but realizing that this was probably the biggest mistake of his life.

• • ⁂ • •

MONDAY MORNING DAWNED, rainy and bleak, with no word from Amadeo. Ellie felt just like the day looked – dreary and dismal and gray. She knew she was likely to see him at the office during the day but how could she face him?

Clearly, the glorious night they had spent together was something he wanted to forget. Why else would he be ignoring her like this? Didn't he know how desperate she was to hear from him?

She couldn't do it. It would be too much, to go into the office, to see him, to see the disdain in his eyes. She would not do it. Not today.

And so Ellie called Vera and, letting her supervisor know that today was not a good day for her, she asked to be allowed to stay home. She was relieved when there was no objection.

Within a few hours, though, she found that there was just so much moping and feeling sorry for herself that she could take. She had to do something.

That something would be to call Rodrigo Castillo. He'd made her promise that if his grandson ever did anything to upset her she would let him know. Well, Amadeo had upset her and she was going to tell. Childish or not, she had an outlet for her anger and she was going to use it.

When she called, Rodrigo was cordial as ever. "It is good to hear from you, Ellie. This warms an old man's heart."

Ellie chuckled. "You're not old." She was sure he knew what she meant. Rodrigo might be advanced in age but he had a youthful spirit that belied his years.

"Sweet Ellie, I appreciate the Monday morning greeting but I have the feeling that you didn't call just to brighten my day. What did my grandson do?"

She drew in her breath then let it out, using those few seconds to gather her thoughts. It seemed none of the Castillos had a problem with beating around the bush. They were so direct, getting to the point without preamble. There was nothing to do but get straight to her story.

"I called because...Amadeo seemed to have disappeared from the face of the earth." She gave a nervous laugh. "Well, not literally but..." she paused, hesitating to tell all, "...after spending a beautiful Saturday evening together he seems to have...dumped me." Despite her resolve to be strong, as she said the last two words her voice trembled.

"He has been avoiding you?"

"Yes, and...I don't know why. I thought..." She was going to say, I thought he liked me, but that sounded so childish. "I thought he enjoyed our time together. I left him a message. He didn't even bother to return my call."

"*Estupido*." Rodrigo growled into the phone. "Still with this 'use them then lose them' nonsense."

Ellie's heart lurched. "What did you say?"

Rodrigo gave a grunt. "It is just nonsense, a stupid saying he's always followed. I am sorry I mentioned it. Maybe that has nothing to do with this."

"You said, use them then lose them. That wasn't Julio's rule, it was Amadeo's." The words came out in a distressed whisper. As the realization sank in, Ellie went cold all over. Amadeo had used her and now he was ready to discard her. In fact, it seemed he already had.

Slowly, her heart sank down until it had settled at her toes. It wasn't Julio who was the cad. It was Amadeo.

"Ellie, let us not jump to conclusions. I will speak with Amadeo."

"No. Please don't. I...I will handle this myself." It was what she should have done in the first place. Why in the world had she dragged Rodrigo into this? "Thank you, *senor*. Have a good day."

"Ellie, wait. You are thanking me? I have done nothing yet."

"Yes. Yes, you have. You have made things very clear to me. Thank you."

When Ellie hung up the phone she sat there on the sofa, staring blankly in front of her, lost in her thoughts. And as the mist began to lift, her heart grew hard and her thoughts grew cold.

Amadeo had used her and then he'd ditched her. He'd had the whole thing planned.

But she wasn't going to take this lying down. He could not stay away forever. When he came back from wherever he'd disappeared to, she would be waiting.

And she would let him know exactly what she thought of a worm like him. She would give him a piece of her mind if it was the last thing she did.

CHAPTER EIGHTEEN

The week in New York went by deathly slow for Amadeo. He had more than enough work to keep him busy so that was not his problem. The problem was, he could not get Ellie off his mind.

No, that was the understatement of the year. He was missing her terribly, so much that he'd spaced out in more than one meeting, losing his train of thought and having to apologize for his failure to catch some important details from the presentations.

The even bigger problem was that he couldn't figure out what the heck Ellie was up to. Like he'd told Julio, he gave her a couple of days' grace and then he'd called her on Tuesday night. The cell phone rang without an answer and then went to voicemail. He left a message, asking her to call him back. She did not respond.

He called again, late that night, but this time he called the phone in her hotel suite. Maybe she had the cell phone off. Maybe she hadn't realized he'd called. He was glad he had another way of reaching her.

But he fared no better with this one. The phone rang eight times before it clicked off. No answer.

Not wanting to disturb her during the day when she would be in the office, Amadeo waited until the next evening to try again. To his chagrin, it was a repeat of the night before – no response from the cell phone or the hotel phone.

And then he grew worried. He called hotel reception but was coolly informed that no, *Senorita* Goldwell had not checked out, and that she was taking no outside calls as she did not wish to be disturbed.

That floored him. Was she actually refusing his calls? Had she gone so far as to advise the hotel not to put his calls through?

Next morning he was on the phone to his Buenos Aires office. As soon as he'd greeted the receptionist he made his demand. "Put me through to *Senorita* Goldwell, please."

"I am sorry, *senor*, but *la senorita* is without access to a telephone where she is. She says she prefers it that way and will call in throughout the day in case we need her."

That was the most bizarre thing Amadeo had ever heard. "Where the hell is she?" he grated. Then, recognizing the inappropriateness of his language, he tried again. "*Disculpeme*. Excuse me. Where is *Senorita* Goldwell?"

"She is in Catamarca. After the final photo shoot there she decided to stay. She is staying with a local family. Unfortunately, they have poor cell phone signal."

That silenced him. It was obvious she was doing her best to make herself unreachable. The only person she could be trying to avoid was him.

His jaw tightening, he growled into the phone. "Get a message to her," he said, trying his best to keep his voice calm. "Tell her to call me immediately."

After a terse instruction like that, Amadeo had expected his phone to ring within minutes. No such thing. An hour passed, then two, until the day ended with no sound from Ellie. *Diablo!*

Amadeo did not call again that day. Neither did he call the day after. When Friday came around he still did not try to reach Ellie. He could have pushed things. He could have demanded that she return to the Buenos Aires office where he could reach her. He did not. When he returned to his Argentina office it would be time enough to deal with Ellie Goldwell.

That Sunday morning he was surprised when he got a call from Julio. "When are you going to be back in office?" his cousin asked. "I need your help on something."

Immediately, Amadeo was suspicious. "What kind of something?"

"You know I'll soon be off for my M.B.A."

"Yes, after the party we held in your honor, I think we all know that."

"Listen to me, will you?" When he got the silence he demanded from Amadeo, he continued. "I want to get the M.B.A., yes, but there's another reason why I want to go to North Carolina."

Amadeo let out an exasperated sigh. This would not be hard to guess. "A woman," he said drily.

"Yes, but not just any woman. It's Maya. I found out she's a professor at Duke. That's why I've registered there."

Amadeo frowned. "Maya? Your old girlfriend from college?"

"That's her. She's a university professor now."

"The same Maya you played that stupid trick on, the one who stormed out of your life?"

"The same one, and will you stop rubbing it in? It was all a mistake."

Amadeo gave a snort. "You can say that again."

"Anyway, stop judging me and listen. I've got an idea I want to share with you, a way I can win her back. I'll drop by your office tomorrow so we can talk. You'll be back by Monday, right?"

"I'm flying back today, but who says I want to spend my precious time on you and your rotten love life? When I'm in the office I'm there for business."

"Yeah, yeah, but I know you can spare your cousin a few minutes. And where do you come off, calling my love life rotten? Last time I checked, yours didn't smell so rosy, either."

Amadeo scowled. "Let's not go there."

"Okay, we won't. But expect me on Monday. I'll be there by ten." Before he could get a response he'd clicked off, leaving Amadeo scowling at the phone.

Monday morning found Amadeo in his Buenos Aires office by seven-thirty. He'd been on pins and needles, anxious to get the day started. He knew he had a lot of work awaiting his attention but the pins and needles had nothing to do with that. It was the thought of seeing Ellie again that made his breath quicken.

There was no denying it. It didn't matter how hard he'd fought, he'd lost not only the battle but the entire war. He'd fallen – no, pitched – hopelessly into love with Ellie Goldwell and no amount of posturing or faking was going to change that fact. The week he'd spent away from her, not being able to speak to her, not seeing her, not touching her, had been the hardest week of his life. Not even when he'd been left alone to fend for himself as a child had he felt so forsaken. He wanted Ellie, needed her, in his life. He knew that now. Whatever his doubts, whatever his fears, he would just have to deal with them.

With the thoughts swirling around in his head, it was no surprise to Amadeo that he did not get much work done that morning. When Maria popped her head in at eight-thirty he hadn't even switched on his computer.

"*Bienvenidos, senor*. We missed you." His assistant gave him a bright smile.

"Thank you, Maria." He paused, not wanting to seem at all eager, but then he gave in to his urge. "Is Ellie...*Senorita* Goldwell...in this morning?"

"Not yet, *senor*. She called to say she needed to make a quick stop before coming to the office."

He nodded. "When she gets in, please send her to my office right away."

"Of course, *senor*. I will do that."

After Maria had gone, Amadeo did his best to concentrate on work while he awaited Ellie's arrival. It was hopeless and that was why, when Maria announced that Julio was there to see him, he did not object. He actually welcomed the distraction. He would accept anything that would keep him from drowning in Ellie's aura, unable to do anything but pine for her.

And that, he had to admit, was exactly what he was doing. Unmanly though it might sound, even to his own ears, he was hopelessly pining for a woman who might have already decided he was not worth the trouble.

"Ready to hear it?" Julio was all smiles as he walked into the office. Not waiting for an invitation, he grabbed the nearest chair and flopped down into it.

"All right. Why not?" His lack of enthusiasm plain in his voice, Amadeo sat back in his chair, waiting to hear what madcap plan Julio had concocted to win his old flame back.

"I've already registered for one of her classes. Managerial economics. She's going to get the shock of her life when she sees me in her class."

"I'm sure." Amadeo's tone was dry.

"Once she sees me, the memories will come rushing back and she will-"

"Welcome you with open arms after, what, eight years? I can just imagine the reunion." Amadeo's words dripped sarcasm but his cousin seemed unfazed. Wanting to knock some sense into Julio, he continued. "She could probably be married, for all you know."

Julio's smile was smug. "I already checked. Free, single and disengaged. I've got this plan-" Suddenly, he paused. "What are you frowning about now? You don't want to hear my plan?"

Annoyed that Julio had noticed, Amadeo's frown deepened. The conversation with his cousin had triggered something in him, had made him think of something disturbing. She could probably be married, he'd told Julio. It made him think of himself...and Ellie...and where they would be eight years down the road, or even one year from now. If he let Ellie escape him now, would he ever have a chance with her again? Or would he lose her forever? He didn't even want to contemplate the possibility. It was that thought that had him scowling.

"It's Ellie, isn't it? You've got her on your mind. That's why you can't hear a word I'm saying."

Amadeo didn't answer right away, gritting his teeth as an unfamiliar emotion welled up inside him. When he looked back at Julio, for the first time in his life he was struggling to find words.

"Yes," he finally said, "it is Ellie. I cannot get her out of my mind. She consumes me. I..." His voice trailed off. This was not like him, this weakling who had fallen under the spell of a woman. But she was a woman like no other. She was Ellie.

Julio began to chuckle. "And what of that decree you made, use them then lose them?"

Amadeo drew in a deep breath and then he shook his head. "I can't. Not with Ellie. Not with the one woman I've ever met who makes me feel whole."

Julio's smile disintegrated and in its place was a look of disbelief. He raised his eyebrows. "*Dios Mio*, she has you by the *cojones*."

Slowly, Amadeo shook his head, the realization finally sinking in. "More than that," he said, his voice low and grave, "she has me by the heart."

•• ❧ ••

ELLIE COULD HAVE KILLED him. After abandoning her, going so far as to leave the country just so he didn't have to see her for the past week, Amadeo was summoning her to his office? So she was supposed to be at his beck and call, to be present when he wanted her, disappear when he'd had his fill but then be there, waiting in the wings, hoping he would spare her another glance? He had some nerve.

And the message she'd retrieved from her cell phone days after his departure did not, in any way, lessen his guilt. He was a heel of the highest order and she would tell him exactly that.

Knowing full well that this might be her last and only chance to ever tell Amadeo what she thought of him, Ellie nodded her thanks to his assistant, straightened her back and stalked off toward his office.

She didn't even bother to knock. Why should she show him the courtesy of a civil entry? Besides, she was too riled up to be nice.

Itching to let him know exactly what she thought of him, as soon as she pushed the door open, stepped in and slammed it behind her the words began tumbling out. "Amadeo Castillo, if you think you can use me then ditch me-"

She stopped. Oh, heavens. He was not alone.

Ellie's hand flew to her mouth, her eyes wide. Who was that sitting in the chair in front of Amadeo's desk, and what had he heard? Then, realizing the stranger must have heard every word, the new question that hit her was, what had the stranger understood?

Mortified, she tore her gaze from the back of the dark-haired head and looked at Amadeo. He was staring back at her and it was obvious he was shocked by her entrance. "I'm...sorry," she began. "I thought you were alone."

And then she heard the soft laughter. It was coming from the man who still sat there, his back to her. As he began to turn around she could feel the color rising in her face.

And then she saw who it was. "Julio!" His name came out in a gasp and she sagged in relief. "Thank God it's only you."

His smile widened. "Only me? I am offended." Of course, he didn't look offended in the least. Then he shook his head. "And what you said just now about Amadeo using you then ditching you, not on your life, honey." He gave her a sly, typical Julio Castillo grin. "The man may have forgotten to tell you this, but he's madly in love with you."

Ellie sucked in her breath. Her heart flipping over in her chest, she swung her gaze back to Amadeo. Was this a joke? "Wh...why did he say that?" She could hardly get the words out. "Did you tell him that?" She held her breath, knowing she would just die if he said no.

And what if he laughed at her stupidity? She would gladly sink into the ground in shame...

The thought was hardly formed in her mind when Amadeo was up and out of his chair and walking toward her. As she lifted her face to gaze up at him, he reached out and placed his hands on her shoulders. He smiled down at her and it was a smile so gentle, so loving, and so tender that it wiped the last shred of doubt from her mind.

His grip on her shoulders tightened. "Every word of what he said is true." His voice was husky and full of emotion. "I was a fool not to tell you this before. I love you, Ellie, more than you could ever know."

Ellie's lips began to tremble. As she gazed up at Amadeo, her eyes began to fill with unexpected tears. Was her sweetest dream coming true?

She opened her mouth to speak but no words came.

"Just tell him you love him so he can kiss you."

They jumped. Ellie and Amadeo both turned to stare at Julio who sat there, grinning up at them.

Immediately, Amadeo jerked his head toward the door. "You may go now."

Julio lifted his hands as if in surrender. "Of course, *senor.* Gladly." He was still chuckling as he got up, sauntered past them and went through the door.

As soon as it clicked closed Amadeo swung his gaze back to Ellie, eyebrows raised. "Now you know how I feel," he said. "And what about you? I know I don't deserve this but could you find it in your heart to love me, too?"

Ellie could not help but smile. It was a soft, tender smile, a reflection of the depths of her love. "I love you so much," she whispered, her voice thick with emotion. "I'm so glad you love me, too."

His smile deepened. "How could I not? You're one of a kind, Ellie, the beauty who has tamed the beast in me."

At his words she moved closer, slid her arms around his waist and pressed her cheek against his chest. And it was wonderful, just resting there, listening to the beat of his heart. This was where she wanted to be.

And, just in case he hadn't heard her the first time, just in case it hadn't sunk in, Ellie tightened her arms around her man and said, with all her heart, "Beast or not, I love you, Amadeo Castillo. Now that I know you love me, don't think you can ever scare me off."

Amadeo chuckled, a deep rumble that Ellie could hear in his chest, and he rested his cheek against the top of her head. "And for that, I thank the stars. You're so beautiful, Ellie, inside and out. You have my love, *para siempre.*

And although Ellie had no idea what those last two words meant she knew that, from this day forward, this beast would be hers for always.

173

Thank you for reading!

Free book offer: Get your free copy of 'Rome for the Holidays' by joining my mailing list. On signing up you will be provided with the link to the story. Just visit my website to join:

www.judyangelo.com[1]

. . ❧ . .

IF YOU'VE ALREADY READ this story and would simply like notification when I have new books out, still visit my website and click on the sign-up link to join my mailing list. You may then choose to ignore the link to the free book. When new stories are out I'll keep you posted. You can also take advantage of *monthly prizes* and *free Advanced Review Copies*.

www.judyangelo.com[2]

. . ❧ . .

If you wish to drop me a line, please send your e-mail to:
judyangeloauthor@gmail.com

.

I would love to hear from you!

1. http://www.judyangelo.com/

2. http://www.judyangelo.com/

BEAUTY AND THE BEASTLY BILLIONAIRE

Sneak preview of the next in the series:

Training the Troublesome Tycoon

The Castillos, Book 2
Julio's Story

Julio Castillo is incorrigible! Smooth, suave and egotistical, he's a danger to any woman who comes within viewing distance. Lady killer? That's an understatement. And it doesn't help that he's a Castillo. Known for their bold and dominant nature, they never know when to take 'no' for an answer.

But when Julio decides he wants his old flame back, he finds that the tables are turned and he's the one fighting for a foothold. **Maya Malone**, once reserved and easy-going, has blossomed into a determined woman who knows how to take control. And, before Julio knows what's happening, she's the one in charge.

This time, it's the fairer sex that's calling the shots!

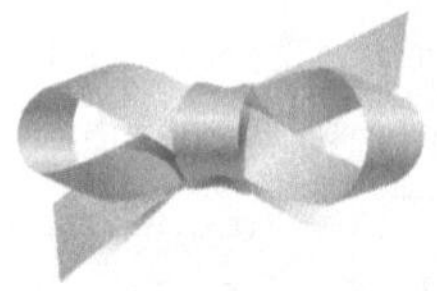

CHAPTER ONE

Murphy's Law – if anything can go wrong, it will. Maya knew it well. That cursed law had been the story of her life lately.

And today was no exception. Today of all days, just when she needed to get into the office extra early, the darned car decided to break down – right in the middle of rush hour traffic. Damn!

It was a good thing she'd renewed her Triple A membership. It took them a while to get to her, what with traffic being so crazy in Durham at this time of year. It was September and, with schools back in session, the roads were packed with vehicles. By the time AAA showed up, Maya was just about ready to pull her hair out.

Before the servicemen could even get out of the truck she rushed over. "Where were you guys? I'm going to be late for class!"

The older of the two men switched off the engine then turned to look at her, his expression one of pure boredom. Clearly, even in the face of her agitation, he was not impressed. "We got here as fast as we could, lady." He glanced down at her hand clutching the top of the door. "The quicker you let go, the quicker I can get out and get started."

Ticked off by his near insolence, Maya frowned but she took a quick step back and watched as he pushed the door open and got out.

She had to fight to keep the expression of surprise off her face. The man was as short as he was insolent. When he'd been in the car she hadn't realized how small he was. For one so diminutive, he certainly had a grand attitude.

The other man – a tall, lanky youth with long, brown hair – hopped out. "What's the problem, ma'am?" He gave Maya a wide smile that made her like him right away.

"I don't know. My Camry was running along as usual, quite well, and then suddenly it seemed to lose power. I only had enough time to pull off the road." Maya frowned as she remembered how the sudden loss of power had scared her. "Maybe it's the battery?"

"Well, that's what we're here for. We'll find out." The youth followed the older man, obviously his boss, toward her car. He climbed into the front seat and turned the key in the ignition. Nothing. "It's dead, all right," he said. "It looks like it's either the alternator or the battery." He leaned forward to pop the hood. Mr. Insolence lifted it and peered under. "Turn it again, Lenny," he yelled.

Lenny obeyed. He turned but again, nothing.

Maya stepped forward, approaching the older man. She had no time for this. She had only twelve minutes before it was time for her class to start and she was still several minutes away from the Duke University campus. "Is it the battery? Can you give me a jump start? Can you just do something so I can get out of here?"

"Patience, lady. We've got to check what's up. How do you expect us to fix it if we don't know what's wrong?" Mr. Insolence was back in all his glory. Just what Maya needed.

"Don't worry, lady. We'll have you on your way in no time." Tall and lanky was smiling at her again. She smiled back at him, grateful for his reassurance. Right then, she needed it.

It took another ten minutes before the men had her engine running again. It was, indeed, the battery. Fortunately, they were fully equipped and were able to install a brand new one in minutes. The only problem was, those were precious minutes she didn't have to spare. She'd had twelve minutes to go when they arrived and they'd taken up ten of them. Now she only had two minutes to get to class.

She hopped into the car. "Thanks, guys. Got to run." She gave them a smile that didn't reach her eyes – how could it, when she was so flustered she'd begun to sweat – and gave them a wave goodbye. Then she was off.

It took her twelve minutes to get to campus but this meant she was already ten minutes late. And, as bad luck would have it, there was no parking spot available. It took another three minutes of driving around before she found a spot. After that, there was only time to grab her leather case off the backseat, throw the strap of her bag onto her shoulder, and race toward the West Duke Building.

When she pulled the door open and stepped in she didn't even bother to be dainty. Instead of being ladylike and cool, she chased up the stairs and hurried toward the classroom. When she pushed the door open, the room was already full of students chatting away, none of them seeming to notice that she was late. Thank God for that.

"Good morning, everyone." As she spoke she was heading toward the desk at the front of the lecture room. She plopped her bag and laptop case on the chair there. "My apologies for being late. Let's get started." She stared pointedly at a group of students who looked like they weren't ready for class at all. They hadn't even stopped chatting when she walked in.

It took a moment of silence, a silence during which she just stared at them, before they turned then sauntered off to their seats. Maya sighed. She'd had a rough morning. The last thing she needed was a bunch of unenthusiastic students. She hoped she wouldn't have to jump through hoops to get them excited about the class.

She forced a smile and turned toward the students. "Why are we here?" She threw out the question and glanced around, searching for an eager face or two.

A small redhead raised her hand. "To learn behavioral economics."

"And what is behavioral economics?" Maya threw back at her.

When the girl looked thrown by the question she glanced around again, searching for another volunteer, not wanting to pressure her first willing student. To her surprise, one of the students who had ignored her entry put up his hand. He grinned.

"A class we have to take if we're going to get our M.B.A.," he smirked, nodding when the rest of the class chuckled and sniggered.

Maya decided to ignore his attempt at snarky humor. "Thank you, but for the benefit of the rest of the class I will use a more traditional definition. Behavioral economics is the coupling of the psychology of decision-making with economic theory. It is the study of how psychology, emotions, society and thought processes influence economic decisions, and the impact all of this has on the society at large." She glanced around the room again. "And who can tell me the value of studying behavioral economics?"

This time it looked like her question had stumped them all. No one was raising a hand. What was worse, whenever she looked at them, many dropped their eyes. Obviously, they didn't want to be called on.

She smiled. "I'll help you with that one. You are here to study behavioral economics because it is the understanding of economics which will give you the competitive advantage in creating value for customers. Many of you might not know this but behavioral economics is a practical science. There are competitors who want the same scarce resources you want, in this case, customers. How much more valuable will you be to your organization if you can understand the psychological and societal value of your product and communicate that so well to the public that customers will come running?" That seemed to get their attention because there was silence in the room and everyone was looking at her intently, including Mr. Smart Aleck. Perfect.

Maya was warming to her subject. "Behavioral economics is really exciting and I'll tell you why. Just imagine-"

"Excuse me."

She glanced up. She gave an involuntary gasp, her eyes widening at the sight before her. There, standing in the doorway, was Julio Castillo, a man she had not seen in almost a decade, a man she'd thought she would never see again.

Giving Maya a respectful nod, he stepped inside. "Sorry to be late," he said and, just like that, he went and climbed the steps at the side of the lecture hall and took one of the seats at the back of the room.

What in the name of Neptune was he doing here? In her class?

Realizing she was staring and would soon be causing raised eyebrows, Maya cleared her throat and looked down at her class materials. "You should have all purchased your textbooks by now," she said, her voice overly bright as she tried to hide her confusion. "Let's turn to chapter one." She flipped open the book on her desk, glad for the distraction, but knowing that there was no way she would get through today's class with Julio Castillo lounging there in the back row, staring at her.

At the first break she would tackle him. Whatever game he was playing would have to end. There was no way she was going to stay in the same room with the man who had betrayed her best friend and ripped out her heart in the process.

· · ∞ · ·

Get your copy of 'Training the Tycoon'
from your favorite online retailer

BEAUTY AND THE BEASTLY BILLIONAIRE

Book 2 - Outwitting the Wolf
Book 3 – Romancing Malone
BAD BOY BILLIONAIRES – WHERE ARE THEY NOW?
Tamed by the Billionaire – THE SEQUEL
COLLECTIONS
BAD BOY BILLIONAIRES, Coll. I - Vols. 1 - 4
BAD BOY BILLIONAIRES, Coll. II - Vols. 5 - 8
BAD BOY BILLIONAIRES, Coll. III - Vols. 9 - 12
BILLIONAIRE BROS. KENT - Books 1 - 4

. . ⊶ . .

Author contact:
www.judyangelo.com[1]
judyangeloauthor@gmail.com

. . ⊶ . .

. . ⊶ . .

---

1. http://www.judyangelo.com/

JUDY ANGELO

Author contact:
judyangeloauthor@gmail.com

. . ⚜ . .

Connect with me on Facebook:
Judy Angelo Author[2]

. . ⚜ . .

Cover Artist: Ramona Lockwood (Covers by Ramona)

---

2. https://www.facebook.com/pages/Judy-Angelo-Author/207657399403357?ref=hl

Did you love *Beauty and the Beastly Billionaire*? Then you should read *Home for the Holidays*[3] by JUDY ANGELO!

DADDY BY DECEMBER

A little girl, a wish, and a woman determined to stay out of his reach. How to reconcile the three?Billionaire investor, Drake Duncan, is at the top of his game. He decides to hire a ghostwriter to work on his memoir. Little does he know that the writer who will answer the call is truly a ghost - from his past.Meg Gracey is the proverbial 'starving artist', a writer down on her luck. When she is offered a contract as ghostwriter she jumps at the chance, only to later realize that the job will throw

---

3. https://books2read.com/u/m0z5OY

4. https://books2read.com/u/m0z5OY

her directly in the path of the man she vowed never to 'touch with a long stick'. Caught between starvation and emotional torture she is forced to choose.Does she follow reason or give in to the desires of her heart?

ROME FOR THE HOLIDAYS

Talk about sexy as sin...Arie Angelis is floored when she lays eyes on the handsome hunk seated at the head table at the holiday event she's catering. She literally can't take her eyes off him. She's always prided herself on being the consummate professional, but not this time. But, attracted or not, when she finds out who he is she realizes he's way out of her reach. But you can't stop a girl from dreaming...Rome Milano is used to getting what he wants but when he meets the hot and heavenly Arie Angelis he learns that he can't always have his way. He's used to calling the shots but, if the lady has her way, not this time...

ROME FOR ALWAYS

Arie Angelis is on top of the world. She's engaged to the man of her dreams, the super-handsome and successful CEO of Belitalia, Rome Milano. She could not believe it when he proposed on Christmas Day. Of course, she said yes! But then, only a month into their engagement there's a turn of events that threatens to steal her newfound happiness. In the past she'd made a life-altering choice. Now it's time to stand by that decision. The only question is, will Rome stand with her or will it send him running?Rome Milano knows a good thing when he sees it and when he meets Arie he has no doubt that she's the one for him. He falls so swiftly in love with her that within weeks of meeting her he's proposing. He can't be any happier when she accepts. But there's just one problem - how to convince the important people in his life that this is for real. Now that he's found happiness will he be forced to choose between love and loyalty?It's decision time on both sides. Through it all, will love prevail?

Read more at judyangelo.blogspot.com.

Also by JUDY ANGELO

Bad Boy Billionaires - Where Are They Now?
Tamed by the Billionaire - The Sequel

Billionaire Bachelorettes of Bel-Air
In Bed with the Enemy

Billionaire Brotherhood
The Billionaire Brotherhood III, Vols. 9 - 12

Historias Multimillionarias para Navidad
Rome para Navidad

KNOWLEDGE in a NUTSHELL
How to Write a Romance Novel

MADE FOR THE MOVIES Fantasy Romance
Trading Spaces
Back from the Future
Back from the Future with BONUS Trading Spaces

Multimillonarios Machos
Domada por el Multimillionario
Domado por el Multimillionario, Bilingual Version

The BAD BOY BILLIONAIRES Series
To Tame a Tycoon
Sweet Seduction
Daddy by December
To Catch a Man (in 30 Days or Less)
Bedding Her Billionaire Boss
Her Indecent Proposal
So Much Trouble When She Walked In
Married by Midnight
Bad Boy Billionaires - Collection II, Vols. 5 - 8
Bad Boy Billionaires Mega-Collection Vols 1 - 12

THE BILLIONAIRE BROTHERHOOD
Tamed by the Billionaire (Roman's Story)
Maid in the USA (Pierce's Story)

Billionaire's Captive Island Bride (Dare's Story)
Dangerous Deception (Storm's Story)
The Billionaire Brotherhood Coll. III Bks 9 - 12
The Billionaire Brotherhood Collection I, Vols. 1 - 4
The Billionaire Brotherhood Double Coll. Bks. 1 - 8

The Billionaire Brothers Kent
The Billionaire Next Door
Babies for the Billionaire
Billionaire's Blackmail Bride
Bossing the Billionaire
The Billionaire Brothers Kent

The BILLIONAIRE HOLIDAY Series
Rome for the Holidays
Rome for Always
Home for the Holidays

The Castillos
Beauty and the Beastly Billionaire
Training the Tycoon
The Mogul's Maiden Mistress
Eva and the Extreme Executive
The Castillos - The Collection

The Comedy, Conflict and Romance Series
Taming the Fury
Outwitting the Wolf
Romancing Malone
Comedy, Confict & Romance - The Collection

The Naughty and Nice Series
Naughty by Nature

Standalone
The Billionaire's Bold Bet

Watch for more at judyangelo.blogspot.com.

About the Author

New York Times & USA Today best-selling author, Judy Angelo, considers herself a 'traveling writer'. She currently resides in Ontario, Canada but prior to that she called New York and then Illinois home. She has also spent considerable time in the Caribbean, Latin America and Europe. She loves to travel as it provides her with interesting and diverse settings for her stories.

Judy fell in love with romance novels as a teenager and has never lost her passion for these stories of love and life, conflict and reconciliation, relationships and family. For her, it was a natural progression from reading romance novels to writing them. So far, she has written over 70 romance novels, including the best-selling Bad Boy Billionaires series. Her other series include The Billionaire Brothers Kent, The Castillos, and the Comedy, Conflict & Romance series.

She hopes to continue entertaining her readers with intriguing stories for many years to come.

Website - www.judyangelo.blogspot.com

I would love to hear from you! judyangeloauthor@gmail.com

Read more at judyangelo.blogspot.com.